OF
CHAOS
AND
FIRE

MEGHAN RHINE

CONTENTS

First published by Chaotic Press, LLC 2023

First paperback edition August 2023

ISBN 9798988991106 (paperback)

www.meghanrhine.com

Cover design by Regina Wamba

Editing by Rebecca Faith Heyman

Proofreading by Red Loop Editing

AUTHOR NOTE

Of Chaos and Fire is an intense, action-packed adventure fantasy, set in a harsh and war-riddled world of elemental warriors. Within these pages, you will find elements regarding war, battle, hand-to-hand combat, blood, intense violence, injuries, and death, all of which are shown on the page. This book will end in a cliffhanger, and references slavery and an arranged marriage. While the burn in this book is slower, and there are no sexual references within, the series progresses in spice and steam. This book is not the standard for heat of the romance and each book gets spicier as relationships develop. Readers who may be sensitive to the mentioned themes, please take note, and prepare to enter a world of chaos...

For my husband, Marlon.
You are my fire. You brighten my darkest days and keep me
cloaked in eternal warmth when the chaos of my own mind
threatens to overtake me.

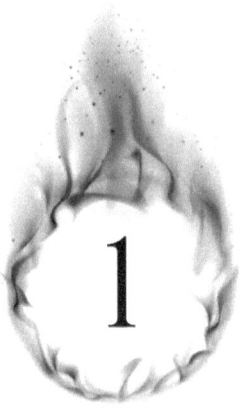

KARA

THE BLISTER-ROUGHENED SKIN OF my frostbitten arm burns bright red through a ripped sleeve. The wheezing of my waterlogged lungs buzzes through the air. Battle has left my fingernails coated in a grotesque mixture of blood and dirt. I scrub it away, desperate to cleanse myself of the sins of war.

"Damn it!" I scream, throwing the soap against my bathroom mirror.

The blood will never wash from my hands. They will never be clean. The souls of the lives I have stolen will haunt me until my dying day, and I will never find peace. The bathroom door flies open with a loud slam. I whirl to confront the intruder.

"*Kara.*" Rae races in, and my fists relax at the sight of my best friend. She throws her arms around me, pulling me into her embrace. "You're okay," she breathes into my hair. "I was so worried."

"I'm all right."

Death has spared me once again, and I can't suppress the niggling guilt at knowing I have found favor with Gaia, who has allowed so many others to fall.

Rae breaks from our hug, pushing me away to get a better look. I know what she sees. The fresh cuts from icicles that barely skirted across my forearm. Peeled skin that could not stand the pressure of a water wielder's stream. The red patches of frost burn that decorate my neck and shoulders, and puffy eyes that failed to hold back tears.

She assesses each new gash in my skin, which will soon heal as scars that lie alongside the dozens of others I've accumulated over the years. I do not hide them. They are a mark of strength, a tally for each battle I've fought and won. But not this one.

This time, the band of warriors I led into battle retreated, serving us no victory. I was among the last to leave the field, joining our faction's remaining warriors in combat until, they too, ran away.

I fought desperately, cursing them as they fled, furious they seemed to have forgotten what we fight for. Hells, with no more to show from this war than a dying faction, I am liable to forget myself.

Caelum.

The Upper holds my cousin captive in their capital, alongside thousands of other Lower elementals. Each warrior is linked to someone lost to the Upper Region, giving everyone their own reason to fight. Caelum is mine; he was among the last of our faction to volunteer servitude to the enemy. He left home in the dying days of our trade agreement, when the Upper demanded greater lengths of service in exchange for marine goods, tech, and the energy to run it. I will not stop fighting until we've retrieved Caelum. I will not run from my enemies until my flesh and blood—the closest thing I have to a brother—is home.

Rae's face softens as she runs the pad of her thumb along my cheekbone, wiping away blood or dirt or, just as likely, both. She winces when her thumb grazes the large bruise circling my eye, as if she is the one who feels the pain. "Oh, Kara."

This isn't the first time Rae's come to assess me after battle. The past few years have been a montage of *goodbyes* and *stay safes.* Rae has seen me off dozens of times, staying back with the rest of our faction members to await our return. I leave pieces of myself behind in battle. Each time my friend receives me, there is less and less left for her to recognize.

I grow increasingly unfamiliar with the woman I've become. The mechanical militant that overtakes me in battle leaves no room for rational thought. The need to fight to the end, to gain any advantage that may bring us closer to recovering Caelum and the others, blinds me. It kept me on the battlefield when I should have led the rest of my band to follow in retreat. In my foolish haze of bloodlust and valor, I only brought more to their deaths.

Rae looks up, remembering to ask, "What about Emi?"

My lips seal shut as my throat tightens. I can't tell her our friend followed me to her demise.

The image of Emi's lifeless body flashes across my mind. I envision her once-bright skin, waterlogged and bubbling, as if she'd spent a decade under that water wielder's stream. Guilt strangles the words that die in my throat. I look down, unable to admit that I could not save her.

I don't have to. Rae knows.

She falls to her knees. "No, no, no."

I crouch down, wrapping her in my arms just as she had done for me. I rock her as she sobs, comforting my friend who could not go into combat. Rae is a Level One fire wielder. She cannot fight in the Regional Battles. For an L1 wielder with no combat experience, it would be sure suicide. As a Level Three, the highest and most powerful of wielders, it's my duty. Just as it's my duty to comfort Rae, to hold back the tears that beg to flood over my cheeks at the massive void our friend's death leaves. To shut down the overwhelming guilt that labors my breathing and pounds against my skull.

I'm our faction leader's daughter. I cannot show weakness, not when my friend is leaning on me for support. Not when I have already failed one.

She hiccups through the tears. "That's what took you so long, isn't it? That's why you and your mom didn't come back with the others."

Her eyes search my face, piecing it all together. Some delay is expected. After each battle, my mom and I stay behind to bury the fallen land wielders. Terras must be returned to the land after death. It's the only way to reunite with our deity, Gaia, who will re-disperse our essence—our lifeforce and the source of our power—to the foliage and soil we command. It took longer for me to bury Emi. Hers had to be special.

For her, I dug my hands deep, searching the soil for a seedling of bilfium stalk. Their leaves are thick and hardy, and the veins that flow through them emit the brightest glow of any other plant. Emi hated the dark, and I wanted to make sure that light always shines upon her.

I wrapped her three times with the burial leaves, doing my best to secure her in the bundle. The thought of insects and other things that crawl through the ground nibbling at her silken flesh turned my stomach. This way, her body will have time to rest before it's returned to the land. It's the least I could do for the friend I failed to protect.

I hold Rae until the sobs no longer choke her and only quiet sniffles shake her chest. I comb my fingers through her curly, black hair. "Let's get you home." Her hooded eyelids begin to close, and her head rests heavy on my shoulder. "Come on, I'll walk you."

I need to get myself out of the house. The cypress walls feel constrictive. Alone with my thoughts, my mind screams at me. It calls me names like *murderer* and *failure*—and I can no longer listen.

My grandmother's cottage is near Rae's, so once I've dropped her off, I make my way over. After the battle I've lost so much to, I only want to curl up on her old sunken-in sofa with a warm cup of spiced tea. She always makes a special brew for me, with sika petals and pilla root. Grandma is a voice of reason, a lifeline to reel me in from the storm of my guilt and insecurities. She has led our faction and navigated through adversity, and I am desperate to find comfort in her sage words and wrinkled smile.

I have not seen her since we last left weeks ago. She stays behind while we go into combat. Not because of her age, but because of her strength. She was our faction's last leader, before my mother succeeded her, and keeps the town safe while we're away. Like me and my mother, she's one of the few Level Threes in our faction, though, her power is tried and seasoned.

I hurry up the steps of her home, freezing once I reach the door. Voices carry through an open window, stopping me before I enter.

"We are losing. They grow stronger while we grow weaker. Soon, we won't be able to defend the faction at all. We must form this alliance." I recognize my mother's voice, stern and strong.

Dad answers. "But is this the best way? Zimara, she's so young. You and I were a decade older before we joined—"

"You and I were not raised in war."

My grandmother speaks up between them. "She still has not accepted her position as your successor. This may be too much on her."

"She is my daughter, and she will lead this faction in the event I cannot. Part of leading is making hard decisions."

"Zimara." Grandma says the name as only a chastising mother could. "She is still young. I'm sure there's another way to secure their allegiance."

"Those were his terms. He wants to ensure his son assumes a position of leadership."

I push the door open before they can continue.

"What's going on?" I say.

My family exchanges glances. Mom fixes her mouth in a hard line. "Have a seat. There's something we need to discuss."

I sit across from my parents, next to my grandmother. Her hand rests atop mine as she gives it a gentle squeeze.

Mom starts. "We barely made it out of our last attack."

She doesn't need to tell me. I was there and know better than anyone. I grimace at the memory of the bloodbath. Each battle returns fewer and fewer of my people, until soon, we won't return at all.

"It's for this reason we've reached out to the Fire Clan's Smithing Faction. It's our intention to form an alliance with them."

"How are we going to do that?" I say, though what I really want to ask is why she didn't reach out to another faction in our own clan—why she sought aid and alliance from a Fire Clan faction. But I know it is my own ridiculous pride. Smithers are superior warriors. They can defend our faction in a way no other in the Terra Clan could.

As we dwindle in numbers and resources, we have little to offer the neighboring faction aside from more of the medicines and elixirs we already trade. I can see the appeal of free access to the Healer salves and remedies but don't understand how it will be enough to warrant the Smithing Faction's aid.

The hard lines of my mother's mouth soften as she glances at the floor, and for a fleeting moment, she seems unsure. The expression is out of place on a woman who's always confident and undaunted.

In the next moment, the gentleness I saw resettles into familiar stoicism as she takes in a breath. "Oryn Stallard has requested a union between you and his youngest son, Cinis Stallard."

Horror runs like ice through my veins.

Dad adds, "And we have accepted, pending your consent."

I jump from my seat, snatching my hand from Grandma's. "I do not consent."

My mother rises to meet me. "The boy will arrive in two days' time. We will accept him into our faction on a courting basis."

I don't care how they accept him. "I don't want to be courted."

"Enough," my mother snaps.

This is not the same soft, kind woman who rocked me to sleep in a hammock of vines. Or blew leaves down from the sky for me to dance in like a spring rain. The burden of war has hardened her. The weight of the faction is so heavy on her shoulders that it has crushed any softness she once had.

This burden, which she wants to pass to me. I cannot bear it. Its weight will kill me.

"This is your faction. You will succeed me when I can no longer lead. The faction will not survive if we don't secure this alliance."

I know the truth in her words. My home is dying at the hands of the Upper. And although my people depend on me, I cannot accept. I have given so much of myself to this faction—this war. I have nothing left. Tears sting my eyelids. She looks from me to my grandmother and father, sighing in something like defeat.

"We will not *force* you to form a union, but you will welcome the pyro into our faction and allow him to court you." The hard planes of her face return. This is the only mercy she will allow me. Still, I shake my head, unwilling to accept.

"I don't want any of this. I don't want him, and I don't want to lead. Find another successor. I'm tired of it all."

Emi races through my thoughts, the last person I led. I couldn't even keep my own band from retreating. I led her straight to death. She was my friend.

"Kara," my grandmother hisses, even her softness receding. Mom's hands ball into fists that glow a faint green, but I don't care about the consequences or their judgment. "You will take your mother's place, just as she took mine."

Dad stands, forming a barrier between the matriarchs and

me. "I know it's a lot, honey, but nothing is final today. Take the next few days to process, and when Cinis arrives, you will accept him."

He lifts my chin as I look away. "Let's take things as they come. You don't need to assume your mother's position at this very moment or marry Cinis immediately. But you must try. You can't run away from your responsibilities. You owe our faction this much, at least." His deep green eyes soften. They are the same green eyes he passed on to me.

My mom and Grandma stand silent, allowing him to talk me off the ledge. He moves forward, pulling me into his chest like a giant bear. I bury my face in his shirt to keep from crying.

"This will be good, sweetheart. You'll see. With the Smithers' backing, the weight we ask you to carry will not be so heavy. A union with Cinis means you won't have to shoulder it alone." He tilts my face back up to look at him. "And if he's an asshole, we'll send him packing."

"Okay," I say, pulling away. I look at the ground as I feel my fate solidifying in place around me. *The only way out*, I tell myself, *is through*.

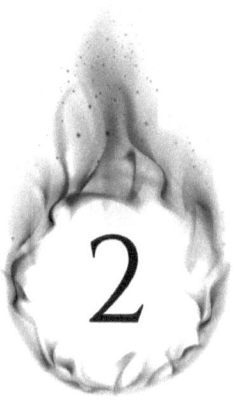

CINIS

I CREEP ALONG THE empty hallway wall, hyper-aware of each step, careful not to make a sound. I ration out slow and conservative breaths so not even the air flowing to and from my nostrils is audible.

The thick, metal door of the armory stands tall and wide, towering above me, begging to be cracked. A vintage lock pad system secures the entrance. It was installed before the Regional Battles, when the Upper traded tech at a cost so high no one could've anticipated the debt we would find ourselves slaves to.

Prior to the initial attacks, most factions—including my own—destroyed all tech the Upper had traded us. We reverted to the more primitive technology from before the Age of Innovation. But some things were necessary to keep—the lock pad and security door included. Although they're among the most advanced machines in our faction, the security system requires constant maintenance.

It's been over a decade since we've traded with the Upper, and with each passing year, the integrity of the machines we kept degrades. This presents its own set of conveniences for elementals, like me, who know their way around the tech.

Today won't be the first time I've broken into the armory. In fact, I've made a routine habit of it. The door's lock pad has a tendency to malfunction, conveniently coinciding with each of my break-ins.

Lifting my palm, I bring it to the security pad, concentrating on the element I command. I draw an electrical current from the surrounding air, as thin and delicate as a strand of hair. It is the same electricity I pull when commanding lightning, only on a much smaller scale. This does not make it any easier, though. I must get the current exactly right to preserve the lock pad. I only need enough to short it. Too much, and the whole thing will blow.

Sweat pools between my brows as my eyes squeeze shut. I focus on regulating the sting pushing at my fingertips, holding back the power until the stab of electricity turns into needles poking through my skin. Pressing four fingers to the lock, I send tiny bolts of lightning in an even pulse until the lights of the pad dim, then blacken. I hold my breath as the steel door bolts release with a clank; pressing my back against the wall, I wait and listen for anyone who might have heard.

When I'm sure no one is in pursuit, I push the heavy, metal slab open, wincing at each creak of its stiff hinges. Once I've crossed the threshold, I scan the room, looking for Turro, the guard and my father's backup solution for the tech malfunctions. The flameater stretches out, asleep on the armory floor.

I roll my eyes. "Useless thing."

This heist may prove to be my easiest yet. Across the armory, displayed in a fire glass case, is the pyrasword. No matter how many times I steal it, it appears no less magnificent. Thoron, our faction's head smith, crafts the priceless swords from pure magsidian. There are no blades sharper and no weapon more equipped to conduct and hone a pyro's flame. These swords go to our faction's leaders.

Beside the magnificent specimen is another—smaller in stature but no less spectacular. This pyrasword is for Lycus, our faction's successor and my oldest brother. The swords are superior to all other weapons in our armory. I train with them as often as I can steal them away. No other blade offers a more precise cut or more balanced strike. It's the only opportunity I have to wield both my element and a weapon so intensely and efficiently. I am a better warrior for it, and although I'll never have a pyrasword of my own, I don't miss the opportunity to sharpen my skill.

I alternate between the two, stealing each just long enough to train. The trick is to get them back in the armory before anyone knows they're missing. If I ever had the chance to earn a pyrasword, it would never leave my side.

My arms reach out for the blade but retract as a rattling hiss fills the space. I halt, not daring to make another move as the hissing grows in intensity. Turro has awakened and is preparing to defend his territory.

I take careful, calculated steps, turning to confront the flameater. Behind me, he holds himself up on four short legs. His long tail and body, tipped with a narrow head and long snout, make him easily one and a half times my size. The scales of his back spike as he lets out a piercing shriek.

I spring into action, snapping my fingers to pull a thick flame from the air. I bounce it from one hand to another, catching the reptile's attention. The shrieking stops as his long snout moves back and forth, following the bouncing flame.

"You want it?" I tease.

The lizard hisses again. I throw the flame into his mouth, and he gobbles it down. When it's finished, he begins to rattle, threatening to let out another shriek. It is a dance we do each break-in. I pull flame after flame from the air, tossing them into the massive lizard's mouth until he is full and satisfied. The reptile retracts his spikes, folding his short legs and rolling over on his back to expose a full-scaled belly. I bend down to rub it, then turn to complete my mission. My hands kiss the hilt of the large pyrasword, my father's. Just as I pull it from the case, a voice calls out my name.

"Cinis?"

My hands drop from the sword. Mom's voice draws nearer. Turro's lazy snout follows me from the floor while I dart across the room, slipping through the open steel door. My pulse quickens. I try to push the door closed as quietly as possible, begging for the old metal to cooperate.

"Cinis," my mother calls again, now even closer than before. The heavy clank of the bolts securing in place rings through the hall as I sprint in her direction, trying to put as much space between me and my father's armory as possible.

"Cinis," my mother says as I nearly crash into her rounding the corner. "Ah, there you are." Her hands grip me to steady herself. "Where are you off to in such a hurry?"

"Just going to train with Xanthe. We need to keep sharp between battles."

Mother presses her lips together, raising a suspicious brow, and I know she will corroborate the story with my older brother later. It's okay—Xanthe is solid, and I can always count on him to cover for me.

"Your father would like a word with you."

So, this is a summons. Mom smiles, but it doesn't reach her eyes. I wrack my brain with all the things Father could be calling to yell at me for. He couldn't have known about the break-in before it happened. Maybe he found out about the custom battle pick I melted in a heated training session last week...

I follow my mom as she leaves. Father is in council with the faction heads. My mother wraps her arm around mine as she guides me from our home and to the meeting hall. She fills the time, picking at my appearance while we walk.

"Cinis, this is pyrite leather." She lifts the broken straps of my charred shirt—another casualty of last week's training. "It'll be weeks before we get another shipment from the Magma Faction."

All pyros need fire-resistant clothing, else we'd likely be a nudist clan. For the terras who live among us, these textiles are as vital as food and water. The land elementals aren't made to withstand a run-in with our fire.

The terras of my faction are hardy and resilient, but the harsh environment my town rests upon isn't hospitable to their kind. Our red sands soak up the sun's heat, holding it and creating a blazing surface that can be dangerous for non-fire-wielding elementals. We've paved most of the town for this reason—to protect others from our natural landscape.

We make our own standard fire-resistant material, but Level Two and Three pyros wear specialty leathers, sewn from the scales of pyrite skin. Those are manufactured by the Fire Clan's Magma Faction, the region's master welders and my mother's native faction. The leather should withstand the highest temperatures, considering pyrites live within magma beds. Much to my mother's dismay, I find myself burning through pair after pair.

We walk the paved streets of my home on our way to the meeting hall. The town's center is abuzz. We've enjoyed a few weeks free from combat, and things almost seem normal.

We pass Lina, who looks over her younger brothers and sisters as they sit in a circle, waiting outside the welding shop for their parents to close for the day. Their matching red hair and freckles leave no room for doubt that they're siblings.

To pass time, the children form teepees of sticks they set ablaze in a game I played as a young pyro. It's a show of power, and everyone competes to grow their fire highest. The smallest girl's fire won't start. All she can produce is a flickering ember as her older brothers and sisters laugh. She's at least a decade away from presenting at her true level.

The youngest of four, I remember how harsh siblings can be. Keeping my hand low and at my side, I pull a flame from the ember in a violent *boom,* quietly drawing the blaze higher and wider until it engulfs all the other teepees.

"*Whoa...*" They all gape at the little girl, none the wiser that she had help.

I smile as she gloats, the apparent winner of this round. Lina looks up at me from where she stands outside the shop door. I press a flirtatious finger to my lips, giving her a wink. The satisfying blush of her cheeks turns a fiery red, just like the silk of her hair. I make a mental note to come back and see her once my father is through with me.

We approach the metal doors of the meeting hall, and my stomach sinks. Pushing them open, I allow my mother to walk through before following her. A fireball crashes against the wall as another dies against an already-charred tapestry. This meeting of heads proceeds just as all the others do: heated. I don't bother wondering what disagreement caused the whole thing to go up in flames this time. It never takes much.

"Cinis," my father's booming voice greets me before we make it to the large, crescent-shaped table, where he sits at the center.

The heads of our faction flank him. My oldest brother, Lycus, sits at his right. Lycus shadows my father at all his meetings, in preparation for the day he will take his place. Father dismisses the heads and elders of our faction. Each files out, one after another, leaving only him and Lycus, while mom closes the door behind them.

Father runs a hand down his long red beard. He does this anytime there's something heavy on his mind. "Son, the Terra Clan's Healing Faction has requested an alliance. One we have accepted."

"That's good news," I say.

I can easily see how we stand to benefit from such a union. The Healing Faction produces the best antidotes and remedies in our region. They specialize in healing, and having easy access to their resources will be beneficial, especially in times of war.

"What do they require of us?" I know it will be protection. Our numbers far exceed theirs, and they have suffered greatly in battle. The question is, how much protection has my father wagered?

His eyes leave mine and drift over my mother and brother. "If the clans continue to stand separately, we will all fall at the hands of the Upper. Zimara Nadir seeks to unite our people by giving us a seat in the Healing Faction's lead family."

"How is she going to do that?" My arms fold across my chest, acting as a shield to keep my stammering heart from bursting through. There are very few ways to enter a lead family.

"We have proposed a union between you and her daughter, Kara Nadir."

My jaw clenches as I try to bite back the questions burning in my throat.

"You want me to leave the faction." It comes out more accusation than statement.

"Yes. You will travel to the Healers tomorrow. If all goes well, that is where you will stay."

I fight to choke back the flames threatening to overtake me. This is my home. The thought of leaving it forever rips me apart. Mom grips my hand, squeezing as if she could pull me from the mess unfolding and take me away from the day that's gone so terribly wrong. I look down at her hand to see it's engulfed in my flames. I retract my fire and try to choose my next words wisely.

"I'm sure you don't mean for me to live there."

"You will marry and lead the faction alongside Kara once she succeeds Zimara." My father's thick, red mustache bleeds into his beard, covering his mouth and curving down with his frown.

Mom turns to look at me as she continues to pat my hand. "The Healing Faction is not very far—only a day's travel. You will always be close to home."

But this won't be home. Not anymore. Lycus finally lifts his gaze to mine before swiftly looking away, speaking up for the first time. "I hear she is very pretty." His voice is low and holds no conviction.

I clench my fists, fighting the urge to hurl a fireball at his face. I stop myself from pulling a lightning bolt down from the heavens to strike him where he stands. Mainly because he is still my brother, and I can't accurately aim my strikes, but more because my father, the only other L3 in the room, stands watching me.

Lycus is the reason he's forcing me to leave. The order stabs at my chest, but I know it's for the good of our people, and I cannot show apprehension. Father chose my oldest brother to succeed him, even though Lycus is only an L2 fire wielder. Ordinarily, this wouldn't be a problem; should an L3 in our faction challenge Lycus for the lead, our family would defend him. We would back his claim to the seat.

But when I presented as an L3, many demanded I be named successor. It is a base principle the factions stand on, that the strongest lead. This situation is unprecedented because my father should not have needed to name a successor before all of his children presented at their full level. Faction leads should have well past middle age to decide who will follow them, but everything changes in times of war.

I know my father navigates this the best way he can. His priority is the faction, and my presence only brings complication.

If I were to challenge my brother, who would back me?

Would my mother stand by my side against her own son?

If Lycus challenges me to negate my claim to the lead, who would stand with him? Would my sister fight against her baby brother?

I don't want to find out. None of us do. That is why I must go.

The thought of leaving my home—my family—twists my stomach, but I do not react. I do not let them see the terror lurking behind my clenched jaw. I must put duty above my feelings. I love my faction, and this is what it needs.

"I accept."

"Very good." My father's smile lifts the edges of his shaggy beard. "We will gather your things, and you will leave at dawn. Azia, we must send him with a gift for his new bride."

The word slams against me like a heat wave. I almost hyperventilate at the thought. Both my other siblings are unwed, though my sister still hopelessly waits for her betrothed to return from the Upper. Lycus is the only one of us married. I look to him—my brother—for some sense of comfort. He only gives me a half-hearted smile.

I have the faintest hope that my sacrifice will not be in vain. That I may gain back the endearment of my brother, who will no longer see me as a constant reminder of his shortcomings—no longer consider me a threat.

I leave the meeting hall to begin packing my entire life into a small carrier bag. Tomorrow, I will leave everything—my home, my family, my freedom—behind for the love of my faction. We all have much to gain, but it seems only I have much to lose.

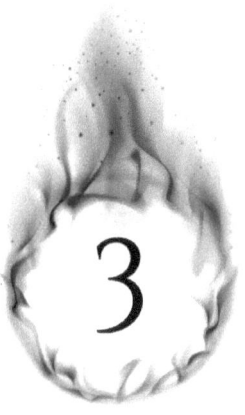

KARA

THE DAY OF CINIS's arrival sneaks up on me. The past two days have sped by, hardly affording me any time to process the fact that the man I am to marry will arrive at my doorstep by sundown.

There's been no hope to change my mother, father, or grandmother's minds, so I don't even bother. Whispers of my betrothed's arrival spread across the faction like wildfire. The town is lively and excited. It's all anyone can talk about—the new alliance, our new guest.

My mother and grandmother busy themselves preparing the faction to accept Cinis. I go to Rae's house, since she's been instructed to make me presentable for my future husband.

She'll weave braids into my hair, pinning back the brown waves that constantly fall across my face.

I only need to knock on the door once before she rushes to open it and ushers me to the center room. We sit atop pillows laid on the floor in front of a large, full-length mirror as we've done a thousand times before. She works through taming my wayward hair, sweeping her fingers across my forehead and pulling back the brown locks that fall across.

"Let's pin this all up so he can see your face." She lights up like a bilfium leaf as she speaks of preparing me for this stranger.

I sigh, waving her off. "Whatever you want to do." I couldn't care less how I look.

Her hands drop from my hair. "I know this isn't exactly what you had planned, but it doesn't have to be a bad thing."

Rae hasn't been able to hide her excitement at the prospect of aligning with a Fire Clan faction. Moments like this leave me longing for Caelum, whose sympathetic ear would have listened as I unloaded my anxieties. He would have been just as apprehensive about this match as I am. I can imagine him scheming to scare the poor pyro off before the end of his first day. Rae, on the other hand, is as eager to meet our new guest as everyone else. As time grows nearer, it seems I'm the only one dreading my future husband's arrival.

"I can't do this. I'm not ready to get married; I'm not ready to lead. Life isn't supposed to move so quickly."

It feels like I'm being cheated, like my life is being cut short by the decisions I'm forced to make.

"I know what you mean. Things have changed..." She drops her hands and looks away.

She fumbles with the comb, and I can tell a secret burns at the bridge of her lips, just begging to be set free.

"What's going on with you?" I turn to look at her face.

My friend hasn't been herself since I returned. Whether it is her way of dealing with Emi's death or trying to grasp at normalcy for the short time we are all home from battle, I don't know. I realize that I have been so wrapped up in my own troubles that I haven't bothered to check in on her. "What is it? Tell me."

Rae bites her lip and stares intently at the comb in her hands. "If I tell you, do you promise not to freak out?"

I nod, not daring to speak in case she changes her mind. She takes a deep breath and pinches her eyes closed. "I'm pregnant."

My mouth hangs in a dumb stare and I gape at her for a few seconds before recovering myself.

"What? When—who?" The questions pour from my mouth the second I can gather my thoughts.

"Not that long. It's still early." She giggles between answering, the warm glow of her fingertips letting me know she's happy. "And... Emrick," she says, as I snatch my hair away, just before her glowing fingers set ablaze.

"I didn't even know you two were together." The tone of my voice decreases to a sheepish mumble. I'm disappointed in myself for becoming so disconnected from my best friend that I didn't even know she was dating an L2 terra I've been fighting beside for the past few weeks.

"It happened right before you all went into battle. I didn't find out until after you were gone."

"Does he know?"

"No, not yet." She pulls her knees to her chest and rests her chin on them, wrapping thin tanned fingers in her thick black curls.

"When are you going to tell him?"

"I don't know. Soon." She buries her face in her knees. I pull her against my chest in a hug.

"A terra, hmm?" I tease, trying to lift her mood. "You're going to be a mom."

Something in me cracks, and I laugh at the absurdity of it.

"Yeah." She laughs back, and the shrill of our uncontrolled giggles turns manic. It may be the only way we're able to cope with everything, and it sure beats the hell out of crying.

As Rae resumes combing and braiding my hair, she tells me about their blooming romance and why she hadn't brought it up sooner.

"You just had so much going on. Everyone has so much going on. It didn't feel right to find happiness in all this chaos, and I didn't want to burden you."

Guilt rides me hard, sitting heavy on my chest at the thought that I've become so reclusive that even my best friend felt she couldn't share this newfound love with me. I do my best to make up for it, letting her gush without interruption about the sweet terra she's totally fallen for.

She retrieves a bouquet Emrick grew for her and weaves its flowers into my braids. The blossoms are full and bright, showing how much effort the terra put into cultivating them. Her smile is giddy and unshielded as she goes on. By the time she has pulled the last strand of hair from my face, I am completely caught up on the relationship and pregnancy.

Rae looks at me through the mirror. Patting her hands against my hair, she adds the finishing touches.

"There. Perfect." She smiles.

I smile back but don't feel the joy I should. The girl Rae sees in the mirror may look like she's prepared to receive a suitor, but I am not.

"Thank you." I give her hand a squeeze and excuse myself.

I should go to my grandmother's house, where a clean and pressed dress hangs waiting. Instead, I find myself wandering across town. I don't know if it's intentional, but my feet refuse to take me where I'm supposed to go. With everything Rae has told me—and everything I'm about to face—I need time to clear my head. When Cinis arrives, my life will never be the same, and I just want to harness one more moment for myself.

I walk until I hear metal slice into wood. *Thump. Thump.* A sound I'd know anywhere. Dad is training.

When I round the corner, an axe glides through the air. Another follows it, then another, each hitting the precise target he aims for. As he releases two more, I throw up a wall of dirt that stops them from hitting their mark. Dad looks up with a smile, pausing his throws.

"Well, don't you look pretty," he teases, and I bring a hand up to the flowers in my hair.

I push the wall of dirt into him, countering his jest. He throws his hand up, blocking just enough so that the dirt crumbles around him, falling on all sides but never slamming into him as intended.

"Picking a fight, I see." He smiles, and I pray he gives in.

I need to get the day's burdens off my mind. I need to fall into the rhythm of combat, let battle instincts take over and release me from any thoughts, save my actions, in this moment. My dad leads our faction in hand-to-hand combat. As an L1, he relies on his skill and weapon more than his element. Caelum is his nephew; Dad trained us both from the time we could walk.

I extend vines from my fingertips, wrapping them around the axes my father has wedged in his targets. I fling them to him, one by one. He catches each with nonchalant ease.

"All right, but just one round," he says.

That's all the invitation I need. I push discs of dirt from the ground and send them flying at my dad. He spins his axes, crushing them as they shoot toward his chest. Another axe comes spinning at me. I dodge it easily as it embeds itself into the tree at my back.

"Looks like you're getting rusty, old man."

I push roots from the ground to wrap around his legs. He

pulls an axe from his belt and cuts them in one swift swipe. The surrounding trees lift their heavy roots, slapping them down—backing away from us—not wanting any involvement in the friendly duel. But one is not quick enough. Dad grabs a branch, extending it to whip across and catch my arm, yanking me forward. I grab control of the shrub, my elemental power stronger than his, and push back, commanding the tree to release me.

It's too late. He's already pulled me close. Dad jabs me with a right hook as I dodge a feint from the left. I swing my leg up to land a kick to his chest, but he catches my foot and twists it.

"Your technique is growing sloppy, daughter." He grunts as I turn and fall to the ground.

While there, I dig my fingers into the soil and command it to open—just a little—beneath his feet. Dad sinks behind me, and I swiftly turn, jumping to stand. Still close enough to command the tree, he grabs ahold of the extended branch and pulls himself out. I order more branches to wrap around his torso and pull him into the air.

Once again, Dad draws an axe from his side, cutting himself down and falling to land on his feet. I push a thick vine through my palm and whip it through the air, aiming it at him. As my whip cracks, he sends another axe soaring, slicing my vine before it can even touch him. As the axe hurls toward me, I move out the way, but not quickly enough. The blade bites into my shoulder as it brushes past me, nicking my skin.

"Damn it, Dad, you got me."

"You still have a ways to go before you can best your old man." He laughs and walks toward me.

I look down to my bleeding shoulder and see the edge of my cut turning a dull black. Dad lines his axes with poison. It's one of my faction's specialties—tonics and toxins. He peeks at my shoulder, assessing the damage

"Come on, kid. Let's get you cleaned up before your mother sees."

The ground trembles beneath us, and I'm afraid he's too late.

"Kara!" I hear my mother yell.

She makes her way into the training area, stopping as her eyes find me and the mess I've made of my appearance. The ground trembles as she glares at Dad, then back at me.

"You were supposed to be getting dressed. Cinis has arrived. Look at you. You're a mess."

My heart stops. It's time. My mind races, scrambling to think of ways to get out of this.

"I can't go now. Dad poisoned me." I point an accusatory finger at my father, sacrificing him to my mother's wrath.

She looks at my cut. Placing four fingers over it, she assesses. "It's a low-grade poison. Your grandmother will tend to it after you greet our guest."

Damn it.

"But Mom, you can't just leave me like this." We both know the minor poison won't do any damage, but it's worth a try.

"Heavens, Kara, your arm will just go a little numb. You'll

live. Besides, you had no business training when you should have been getting ready. Now come on, let's go."

She takes my arm, pulling me from the arena. Dad follows us to the center of town, where she drags me to meet my match. My feet feel like lead and seem to resist my command to move forward. When we arrive, my eyes fall on the crowd of people surrounding my grandmother and *him*.

His dark obsidian eyes peek down at me from under thick, golden curls. His gaze lingers on mine, and his full lips spread into a generous smile.

I draw my hand to the out-of-place braids coated in leaves and dirt. I run a mental check of all the rips in my wrinkled clothes and scratches across my dirty skin. Suppressing the anxiety and self-consciousness that threatens to paralyze me, I meet the gaze of the man I am to marry.

The courtship has begun.

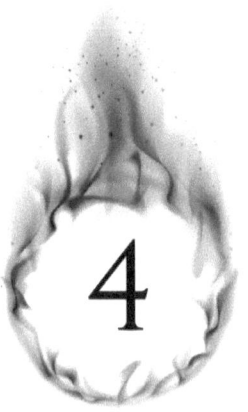

CINIS

THE DAY BEFORE I left for the Healing Faction, I said my goodbyes and wandered around my home, seeing everything for what felt like the first and last time.

I'd taken for granted the burning red sand that coats the Smithing Faction, the constant ringing of metal and fire. My whole life, I've been surrounded by people I know and love, with allies that have supported and protected me since birth. Today, I travel to a place where I have no one.

It was difficult to say goodbye to the friends I've fought alongside since childhood. To look at the place where I've made a lifetime's worth of memories and pack it away into small pockets of my mind to hold on to and open back up when I miss home the most. I walked through our family dwelling, but it had already started to feel distant. Though I know I'll make frequent visits, this was the last time it would truly be my home. My family was quiet. When goodbyes hold so much sorrow, there isn't much to say. Mom and Xanthe, my older brother, helped me pack.

"Here, take this." He discreetly handed me a pyrite suit stolen from our oldest brother while our mom folded more clothes into my travel sack. Only an L1 pyro, Xanthe didn't have any of his own to give me. "I know it will be harder for you to get pyrite leather among the terras, and I'm sure you've burned through all of yours."

He punched my shoulder as I took the clothing from him. The leather folded on itself as I clutched the gift to my chest. The Terra Clan has little need for the specialty material, so the Magma Faction doesn't regularly trade with them. Xanthe and I both know it could take months to get more pyrite leather once I'm among the Healers.

"I'm going to need another brand when you come to visit." His voice was too light as he searched his arms for an empty patch of skin. He'd tried to cheer me up, but his words stabbed at my chest, reminding me I will return to our home as a visitor.

At some point my sister, Kenna, came to stand in the doorway. "And where would he put another brand?" she asked.

"Between the two of you," she waved a hand at the raised lines decorating my flesh. "We might as well just soak all your skin in magma and be done with it."

This is the most she's said since receiving the news of my engagement. Her words sound angry, but her sunken, onyx eyes and down-turned lips tell me she was only hurt. Our father had rejected her own engagement years ago. I think she still blames him for her beau's capture.

Xanthe laughed, determined to lighten the mood.

"I've still got some skin left," he said, gazing at the dozens of brands I've burned into his arms and legs. I'm the only pyro Xanthe has ever let brand him. In my clan, brands are a sign of strength and skill for both the artist and subject. Pyros' skin is naturally resistant to heat, so only a trained Level 3 can wield a fire hot enough to mark it. It bears an unusual pain for an elemental who's never been injured by fire. With dozens of my own brands, I never miss an opportunity to show off my abilities.

"Yeah, I think the only skin I have left to work with is on your face," I laughed. My mom's eyes widened. Xanthe didn't miss the opportunity to torment her further. "Or on my left butt cheek," he said. "There's this girl I've been—"

"Xanthe Kryton Stallard," my mother hissed as the three of us burst into laughter.

Shaking her head, my mother shooed me out of the room, reminding me that there was still much for me to do before my departure.

Lycus had been scarce, avoiding the family since Father gave the directive for me to leave. Sweat slickened my clammy palms. I pressed them into my tightening chest as if they could soothe the coils of anxiety winding around the idea that Lycus might not seek me out before my departure.

I left my room and headed to the armory. Father had given me clearance to collect gifts for my new family—our new alliance. The Smithing Faction is known for its exemplary weaponry. Our production has dwindled since losing the Gold Faction's regular supply of metals. They are our region's mining faction, and the only faction to ally with the Upper in the Regional Battles. It is an exceptional gift, considering how scarce weaponry is becoming. I pulled from the store of implements I had created with my own hands, choosing something for each member of my new family based on the limited knowledge I had of them.

The magsidian we forge from is precious and unique to our faction. We partnered with the Mining Terras, who supplied the magnetite and helped us blend it with obsidian from my mother's faction. Now all we have left is what we repurpose from old blades, and the help we receive from the terras in our own faction. We forge these weapons in pure magma. The joint effort still produces the sharpest blades in the entire realm—gifts my betrothed and her family would surely appreciate.

The armory door creaked open, and though I was there legitimately, my body still jolted, ready to escape. I turned, expecting to see my father. Instead, my mother slipped into the room with me, clutching something to her chest.

"I wanted to give these to you before you left." She moved toward me, holding out two necklaces. "It's obsidian from the volcano of my home faction."

I recognized the two large pendants, which have hung on the obsidian necklace Mom has worn since before I was born. She removed two stones for my brother when he married Lana.

She continued, "I hope you will give one to your future bride and, on the day you marry, fashion them into the rings that will bind you." I took the large stones, grateful for the piece of her I would get to keep close.

"I remember leaving my home faction to marry your father." She looped her arm into mine as we walked from the armory.

"I was so frightened. I had no idea what I was doing or what was expected of me. I felt like my life was ending, that I was leaving everything behind. But then I came here and made life anew. That is the magic of fire wielders: we truly understand rebirth. The rest of the realm thinks our element brings only chaos and ruin, but we know better. We know that only utter destruction affords the opportunity for new life."

She stopped, then turned to look at me. Pulling me down, she raised to her tiptoes, and placed a kiss on my forehead.

"My baby, my sweet baby boy. You cannot know how it pains me to see you go. But I'm sure this is a suitable match, and you will thrive in the Healing Faction. You'll build yourself a new life there and be happy." She smiled at me, and in that moment, I almost believed her.

We continued to stroll together, talking about nothing in

particular. We were to meet with the rest of my family for final goodbyes. On our way, the light tap of tiny feet was closely followed by the sweet voice of my niece, Xuri.

"Uncle Cin." She ran to me, catapulting herself into my arms. I caught her as she let out a high-pitched giggle.

"My sweet Xuri, I'm so glad you're here." I hugged her against me.

"Papa says we have to tell you goodbye today. Where are you going?" she said, pushing herself back from our embrace.

"I have to go away for a little while, but I'll come back to visit. I'm going to stay with the terras in the Healing Faction."

Her tiny button nose crinkled. "The terras? They talk to trees. Why do you have to go there? They're so boring. And they always get into a fuss when someone burns their plants." She folded her little arms against her chest, demanding answers.

"Well, I have to go to make friends with them. So they'll let us use their medicines."

"But why do you have to stay there?"

"Because I'll be marrying a girl there, just like your mommy and daddy got married."

Her eyes lit up with the spark of some new revelation. "And will you have a little girl like me too?"

I nearly dropped her.

"No," I sputtered.

Starting a family hasn't even crossed my mind. This marriage is more than enough for now. Recouping myself, I hugged her tight against me.

"You're the only little girl for me."

She nodded, seemingly satisfied, and wrapped her arms around my neck, squeezing tight. "I'm going to miss you, Uncle Cin. Please come back soon."

"I will. I promise."

I set her down, and she ran to her mother. Lana lifted her up, straddling Xuri on her hip. The little girl wiggled for space against Lana's growing belly. My entire family gathered in the center room, all prepared to say their goodbyes. Xanthe and Kenna came first. Their warm farewells and promises to visit sparked hope that the next few months wouldn't be so lonely.

"You must bring her here for the Lantern Festival," Kenna said as she squeezed me in her arms. "I know she and I will be great friends."

Mother was still tearful, and when she hugged me, I feared she wouldn't let go. I looped both necklaces around my neck, where they'll stay until I'm ready to give one to Kara.

I gave Xuri another kiss on the forehead and placed my palm on Lana's full belly. "May Pyris bless you and my brother with a strong and healthy baby."

My sister-in-law reached her free arm around me. "I will see you before she does. We will send word the moment labor begins."

Lycus looked me in the eye for what felt like an eternity. For a moment, his scrutiny tempered my relief that he'd shown up at all. "You will be missed, brother."

Simple. Short. But it was all I needed. He grabbed my forearms, pulling me into a hug warmer than any we'd shared since I was sixteen years old. Since I presented as an L3. I silently prayed to Pyris that my departure would go some way toward rebuilding the brotherhood that was rattled so severely when I presented. Softly pushing me away, Lycus squeezed my shoulders in a final farewell. I moved on to my father.

"You will make us proud, son. You'll do great things for our factions, I'm sure of it." He pulled me in for an embrace, his thick beard clouding my vision for a brief moment.

They saw me to the door and to my glider just outside. The glider was one of the few "non-essential" pieces of tech left in our faction. When the rebellion began, everyone had burned the Upper's tech. We'd thrown machines and gadgets into the flames of our offering pyres. We'd heated them until the hunks of metal liquefied, flowing like small, silver rivers from the center of town.

It had been a final act of defiance, to reject the very things that brought our people to their demise. To destroy the abominations that made us expendable. But when I found this glider years later, rusting in an abandoned storage building, I couldn't turn it in. Revolutions aside, someone yells "bonfire," and I'm the first in line to burn some shit. But not this glider.

I fought everyone in my family and each of the faction heads to keep her, and damn it, she would go with me to the Healers too. I pressed my hands into the head of my transport. They sank in slightly to give me total control. She revved to life as I jolted little bolts of energy to the power source, and I pulled off, leaving my family behind. I didn't look back as I crossed out of my faction. I knew if I did, it would be in sadness, and that's not how I wanted to remember things.

My glider carried me across the desert sands of my home until the sand exchanged itself for green grass and rich shrubbery. I let the speed clear my mind, losing myself in the drive, not allowing myself to think too far ahead.

A thick tree line comes into view. I've reached my destination faster than I expected.

I'm here now, come what may.

Two colossal trees stand like massive columns at the faction's opening. Their trunks, easily the girth of a small armory, tower impossibly high, dwarfing me as I pass through. They bend to examine me, and I'm sure I will never grow accustomed to sentient flora so massive. Back home, the most our terras could grow were small shrubs and rooted vegetables. The trees lower their branches to graze along my glider, slowing me to a stop. My breath catches once I enter what looks more like a garden than a town.

Two watchmen greet me and escort me through the city. Curious eyes peek out from every direction, and we amass a group of followers as I'm escorted toward what seems to be the faction center. Around me, the assortment of color in this new landscape seems obscene compared to the monochromatic terrain I'm accustomed to.

While the watchmen lead me closer to the heart of the city, a massive statue emerges from the flora. Clearly a tribute to their deity, Gaia, the towering depiction of a full-figured woman with a mother's smile centers the town. They composed it entirely of foliage, its bushes and branches shaped to perfection. Smaller shrubs stand before her. It is a representation of Gaia looking down at the elementals she's granted immortality to, so they can become the terra guardians of our realm.

My faction has a similar tribute made of glass in our own city center. It honors Pyris and her blessing of pyro guardians on our behalf. As I admire the idol, an older terra woman comes out from the crowd to meet us.

"Cinis Stallard, what a pleasure it is to have you here in our faction. My name is Corinth. I am Kara's grandmother and the previous leader of the Healing Faction." She grips my hand.

"The honor is mine." I bow to her.

A crowd gathers around us, and I see my arrival has been much anticipated. Her eyes draw away from mine, looking into the distance, far past me.

"There she is." The wrinkled corners of the woman's mouth curve up. I turn to see she's looking at three figures emerging from the woodlands, reaching her hand out to them as they draw nearer.

"Cinis, this is my daughter and our faction leader, Zimara, and her husband, Quarris."

They've nearly made it to us. Zimara and Quarris walk close together, forming a barrier, while I assume it's Kara who treads behind them. Upon approaching, they naturally begin to part, as if they are revealing a well-kept secret.

"And this is my granddaughter, Kara."

She stands before me, her hair a tangle of thick, brown waves coated in dirt. Red marks line her neck and arms, and smudges of mud streak her face and chest. The shoulder of her shirt hangs open to reveal a nasty cut dripping blood. She looks a complete mess, and I find myself totally enamored.

Her mother is the first to move forward. "Welcome to our faction. I am Zimara."

"I am Quarris." Her father extends his hand to me.

They stand for a long moment, watching me expectantly before I realize I've forgotten to speak.

"Yes—yes, I'm Cinis Stallard of the Fire Clan's Smithing Faction." I bow, rising so quickly it seems spastic, yanking the satchel from my back a little too hard. "I've brought gifts."

I fumble around the bag, removing the weapons with such awkwardness I'm sure I'll cut myself before I've had a chance to distribute my wares.

"These weapons are made of magsidian," I say, pulling myself together, handing each person their offering.

To the grandmother, I give a dagger. Zimara gets a sword.

"I hear that you are quite the axe man," I say to Quarris, handing him two custom battle axes.

His face lights up, and his eager hands grip the weapons. "A man after my own heart," he says, swinging them with a ferocity that causes me to step back.

Lastly, I pull out the orbises, disk blades made only by my

faction. "And these... are for you." I hand them to Kara, whose eyes flash open in an excited flicker. She readily takes them in one hand, holding out the other for me to shake.

"Thank you. It's a pleasure to meet you," she says.

I take her hand into mine, bending down on a knee, channeling all the charming swagger I possess.

"The pleasure is mine," I say, allowing honey to lace my words. I bring her hand to my lips, placing a kiss on the back of her palm.

A sharp sting bites into my flesh, and I drop Kara's hand as if it's a venomous snake. I glance from the blood trickling down my fingertips to the thick thorn slowly retracting from Kara's palm.

"Kara," her mother hisses, tiny pebbles trembling at her feet.

My betrothed is a wild one.

A laugh rumbles in my chest, and I think this may have been a good match after all.

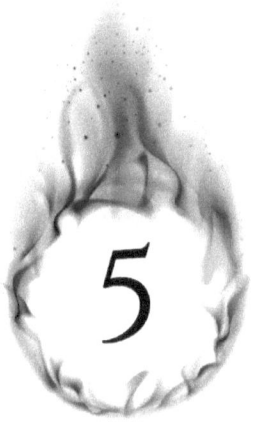

KARA

I SPEND THE NEXT few days playing hostess, hoping my cooperation will abate Mother's fury. Fortunately, Cinis seems to be a good sport, never bringing up the initial thorn incident. I wonder if I'd gone too far by stabbing him, then chastise myself for even caring. Mother spared me no harsh words after the episode, and I feel I've paid my penance.

Although Cinis's lips on my skin weren't entirely unpleasant, they were uninvited. I won't allow him to think he can take such liberties with me. He is not my husband yet. I still belong wholly to myself and will not let him cheat me of the time I have left.

I'm supposed to acclimate him to the faction but have hardly spoken to Cinis in the week he's been here. Aside from the necessary niceties, I find that I have nothing to say to the man I will soon call husband. Upon arrival, he moved into my grandmother's home, where she'll host him as the faction's honored guest. I'm grateful for such small mercies. I couldn't have coped with him living with us too.

Thankfully, Mother hasn't pushed Cinis on me. I will admit that stabbing him probably wasn't the warmest or kindest reception, but he caught me off-guard when he dropped to one knee.

The entire town seems taken by him. I can tell he's doing his best to settle into the faction. Any time I take him out to show him around, he draws a crowd. It's never long before a new group of elementals sweeps him up with questions and special requests for a demonstration of his L3 pyro tricks. Whether he's playing a game of blaze ball or wielding his flames to tell a fire story, there's always a crowd watching him. Sometimes, I stay and watch too.

Today, my mother has asked me to show Cinis the greenery, where we grow all our medicinal and noxious herbs. I resolve to use the opportunity to get to know the pyro a little better. A wise leader would learn as much as she could about a stranger before accepting him into the faction and allowing him to lead at her side. It is the least I can do for my people.

When I make it to Grandma's house, she tells me Cinis left early this morning. It takes a bit before I can locate him.

Just outside the woodlands there's a low peak that overlooks a clearing in the forest. I see him there just as the sun begins to rise into the sky.

He is alone, consumed wholly by his fire. He moves as if he's the force that coaxes the sun from its nighttime slumber. I watch his arms glide through the air as he maneuvers his body to whip and strike like the blaze that engulfs him.

I find myself mesmerized by the dance, hardly able to look away. It takes me a significant amount of time to realize this isn't a dance at all. With each whip of flame, Cinis strikes with a punch or kick. He is training for combat, deadly in his precision and speed.

I find myself moving closer to get a better look, appreciating his flawless technique. As I peer down, his dance changes. The swift combat style moves to the ground, where he sweeps a fiery hand across the floor. He leaves behind clean, curved lines and swirls in the clearing. When he finishes, I see the movements were not sporadic. Far from it, in fact.

When the blaze dies down, the scorch marks left behind form a pattern in the shape of a rose. Cinis turns to look directly at me. A smile spreads across his lips, deepening the dimple in his strong chin. I flush, embarrassed that I've been caught. No point hiding in the shadows any longer. I've been found out. I rise with as much dignity as I can muster and walk down from my perch.

"I wasn't spying." I feel like I owe him an explanation.

"I'd be happy if you were," he says with a smile.

I press my lips into a scowl, not knowing how to take the comment. "My mother wants me to show you the greenery today."

"I'd like that very much."

Having nothing else to say, I turn and begin to walk.

He jogs behind me to catch up. "How far away is it?"

"Just outside the town. Maybe an hour's walk."

"Then I have a better idea." A devilish grin plays across his lips. "Let's take my glider."

I know what gliders are, although no one in my faction has one. I was much younger when our people destroyed all the tech given to us by the Upper. Even before, we traveled through transporter pods. Our area is littered with machines and tech long dead. Rusted metal peeks from beneath moss and overgrown shrubs. Branches poke from controller boards and out of pod windows.

"You kept some of their tech?" I don't mean to sound so accusatory, but the boldness of it is mind-boggling.

He throws his hands up in a mock surrender. "Look, I destroyed everything else. But when it came to the glider, I had to put my foot down. Come on. Let me take you for a ride."

I think of my resolution to learn more about the pyro, but my gut twists at the thought of trying to drum up petty conversation over the hour-long walk. The glider seems to be something he genuinely loves. Surely going for a ride counts as trying to get to know him. "Fine."

"Great. Follow me."

I struggle to keep up as he races ahead.

When we arrive, I find myself fascinated by the strangely shaped transport. Although my fingers drift to the smooth metal, my feet remain grounded in place, refusing to take me closer. The buffed magnetite shines bright in the morning sun, and I wonder what it would be like to fly through the greenery, moving faster than a racing fern cat. Cinis looks at the shiny, bean-shaped hunk of metal as if it's his first-born child.

He swings a leg over and settles into position. The metal sinks beneath his hands, contouring to them. Thin, blue strands of lightning pulse from his fingertips, and I stifle a gasp. The glider lifts from the ground with an audible hum. Cinis holds out a hand, bidding me to jump on. I grab it as he pulls me up.

"There." He secures me behind him. "You're going to want to hold on tight for this."

I drape my hands across his abdomen, barely touching the fabric of his shirt.

He smiles back at me. "So, that's how you're going to play it?"

And before I can answer, he propels the glider forward. I nearly fall back from the force of it. Had he not wrapped his free hand behind him to hold my back, I might have slipped. I lunge forward, gripping on to him for dear life as he laughs and mumbles something like, "That's better"—though his words get lost in the wind.

The ride is thrilling and terrifying, exhilarating and

heart-stopping. I don't know whether I want to get off or speed ahead, so I only clutch Cinis tighter. We ride for a bit before he turns and yells through the wind, "So, where are we going?"

And I remember that he has no clue.

"Keep going in this direction. Cut past that bend and into the clearing."

It takes no time to get to the greenery. As a massive field comes into view, even Cinis knows we've arrived at our destination. Rows and rows of medicinal and poisonous plants expand before us. A shift of terras is already working the crops, tending to them and harvesting what is ready. When we come to a stop, Cinis removes his hands from the glider's head, powering it down. As it lowers, he hops off and reaches his arms out to help me.

"I'm fine," I say, pulling the soil beneath me to form a step as I slide off.

He looks out at the vast field. "So, this is where the magic happens?" And I smile because that's kind of a funny way to put it.

"Well, yes. I guess." I lead him further in. "This is where we grow most of the plants and herbs used in our tonics. Just about everyone in town takes a hand in tending to the greenery. Of course, all the terras rotate out managing the plants, but there are a few pyros that live in our faction."

"Yes, I believe I've met them all," he says, his voice hollow. I can only imagine how lonely it must feel for him, dropped in a new place where there are so few of his kind. A pang of regret wiggles into my chest. I shouldn't have made his stay any lonelier than it has to be.

"The pyros play an important role in maintaining the greenery. Something you may want to participate in is the pre-harvest burning." I try to find something that may spark his interest and lift his spirits.

"You allow the pyros to *purposely* burn your crops?" He folds his branded arms across his broad chest. "I wish the terras of my home faction had been such sports."

"The burning is purposeful. We burn some of the straw, wheat, and stalk crops. It gets rid of the non-harvestable materials while killing microorganisms and enriching the soil." I guide him down the endless rows of blooming and vining plantlets.

"The pyros also help by protecting the greenery. They stand watch and guard it. The destruction of our greenery would debilitate the faction, so their task is vitally important."

He smiles with a nod, and I can only hope it gives him purpose knowing that, although they are few in number, the pyros of our faction contribute greatly to its overall success. Guilt-ridden, I do my best to put on a slightly friendlier front as I show him the heart of our faction. Bringing my hand to latch inside his folded arm, I guide him down each row, explaining what it grows and how it's used and harvested.

"So, this is poisonous?" He gestures to the zelem leaf.

"Yes, it's one of the deadliest plants we cultivate."

He pulls his hand back as if the shrub is a vine viper, coiling to attack. "Then how do you harvest it?"

"It's not harmful to the touch. Most of our poisonous plants aren't," I say, stroking the sapling. "They're even somewhat safe to eat, although I wouldn't recommend it. As terras, we can extract the toxin from the plant material. The same with our medicines. We can identify the genetic makeup of each plant and manipulate it however we please." I gently coax the flower's budded tip to open, exposing its black petals.

"This is why a special subset of terras oversees the manufacturing of our medicines and toxins. They spend a considerable amount of time going through poison study and have particular gifts in making the tonics we need. My grandmother heads it." I try to subdue the prideful smile pulling at my lips.

"She's been the most gifted healer for generations, and my mother isn't far behind her. Then again, I suppose that's to be expected when you lead the Healing Faction."

"What about you?" He looks down at me, giving my arm a gentle squeeze.

"I hold my own," I say, brushing a xanthium with my fingertips, then looking to him. "So, tell me about your faction. Do you have anything like this?"

His obsidian eyes gleam, then dull, marking the high and low emotions behind them. To see the mention of his faction brings such joy and pain stabs at my heart.

"Yes, the core of our faction is the armory. The Smithing Faction is known for its weaponry. We—they—produce the finest in our region." He looks down, and I can tell he's saddened at the mention of a faction he no longer belongs to.

"My father keeps a personal armory in our family home." The corners of his mouth curve into a smile that is deep and roguish, and I can only guess at what mischief lies behind it. Thinking of Caelum, I wonder what my cousin would have to say about the charming fire wielder. I long for his approving nudge, telling me it's all right to succumb to the pyro's charm, just as everyone else in the faction has.

"So, you craft weaponry?"

The smile still plays on his lips. "I made all the gifts I presented to you on the day of my arrival." His chest puffs a bit at the boast.

I think of the odd, circular blades he gifted me. I've hardly been able to put them down, sneaking about every chance I get to have a turn at wielding the strange weapons. But no matter how hard I try, I can't figure out how to use them. "And my gift... what exactly do you call it?"

"Those are orbises. They're a weapon we rarely trade. I thought it'd be fitting for you to have a set. I know you will be deadly with them."

"Maybe to myself. I haven't the slightest idea what to do with them."

"You wouldn't. Only my people are trained to wield them. I suppose you'll just have to let me teach you." He moves closer to me, a wicked smile playing across his lips.

I think I may just take him up on the offer.

CINIS

W E RIDE BACK INTO town to retrieve the orbises. Once I'm sure she won't sprout a thorn to stab straight through my gut, I miss no small opportunity to speed ahead, forcing Kara to dig her fingernails into my abdomen and clutch on to me for dear life. The scenery whips by us in a blur as I push my glider faster. Kara's unshielded laughter tickles my neck, and my only regret is that we make it to the training arena far too quickly.

When we arrive, she doesn't let me help her off. Once again, she pulls the ground to meet her, forming a pedestal to step down from the transport. She leads me into the arena for our one-on-one practice session. There, she unpacks the ring blades with such care and reverence that I am honored to have given them to her. She holds on to their hilt, which runs through the center of the sharp magsidian rings.

"Here. You want to grip it at the center, letting one side rest atop your forearm and the other extend past your fist." I adjust her hand on the hilt. "Very good," I say, as she holds an orbis in each hand.

"When you fight with these, you need to keep an open stance. This blade's advantage is that it's deadly from all angles, as you should be also."

I move behind her to carefully rest my palms on her hips. When she relaxes under my grip, I pull them back to open her frame. She stiffens at the movement, but then loosens, allowing me to mold her into the proper fighting stance.

"Good. When you strike, you must take care to keep your arms out. Never allow the blade too close to your own body." I spread her arms. In one fluid motion, with my hand still resting under her forearm, I sweep down. "Like this."

She leans into me as I do the same with her other arm, gently pulling it back to demonstrate the panoramic striking capabilities of this weapon. Her body stills against mine, and I believe I've taken too many liberties. Kara's voice is barely above a whisper when she turns her head up to look at me.

"Thank you, but I think I have it from here."

And I stand back, because I have no doubt she does.

Her first moves are slow and calculated, acclimating herself to the round blades. She takes care not to nick her forearm as she cuts into a practice bag. Her movements start a little spastic, but the way she wields the orbises is impressive for a first timer, and I shudder to think what a force she will be after some practice.

"Stand back," she says as she twists and slices through the practice bags surrounding her.

I comply immediately, and am glad I did, because no sooner do I move back than I see her push green vines from her fingertips. They wrap around the orbises' hilts, pushing them far past her arm's reach. She twists the blades, spinning them in a deadly, fan-like motion. As they swirl in the air, attached to the ends of her vines, it doesn't take long for them to tangle into each other and fall to the ground. I know in time she'll be the deadliest wielder of these orbises, and I could not be more proud.

"I've never seen that done before," I say.

"You haven't seen anything yet." A sly grin creeps across her lips, and I think it's the first time I've seen her mouth curve that way. She bends over to retrieve her blades as a young terra boy comes into the field.

"Yield! I have a message to deliver!" he yells. "The faction meeting has begun, and the heads request your presence."

"Damn it," Kara mutters. "I'd completely forgotten. Let them know we'll be right there."

The boy nods and takes off, running to deliver the message. It's this archaic form of communication that makes me miss the tech I grew up with. Tech like comm units, which allowed us to communicate remotely. While we still have telecoms from before the Age of Innovation, our lack of power to run them often renders the devices useless. With each passing year, the Lightening Faction struggles more with distributing power to the region. Without coal from the Gold Faction, we will soon receive no power at all.

Kara packs away the orbises with as much care as she unloaded them. Once finished, she leads me into town, where the faction meeting takes place. On our way there, she briefs me on their table of elders. Each faction has one, comprised of the heads of the factions' most prominent families. The table acts as a check to the power of the faction lead.

Once we make it to the meeting hall, we do our best to sneak in unnoticed through the back door.

"So good of you to finally join us, Kara," an elder says.

Zimara glares at the board member. "You two take a seat. We were just discussing our plans for another retrieval."

My spine straightens as I hear the words. Alarm bells go off in my head, but I try not to show it. They mean to retrieve some of the faction members they traded to the Upper before the war.

Years ago, the Upper and Lower regions coexisted somewhat peacefully. The Upper provided most of our energy, technology, textiles, and marine goods. While trading with them enhanced our quality of life, we were wholly autonomous. Our region was self-sufficient, while the Upper suffered, needing our medicines, vegetation, welding, and smithing trades.

During the rule of Prime Policymaker Nero, the region made several technological advances. No longer the struggling region they'd been only a few years prior, the tech he introduced essentially rendered the Lower elementals obsolete.

With tech that could perform many of the tasks and produce much of what the terras and pyros could, the Upper no longer needed to trade in the traditional sense we always had. They took advantage of our eagerness to gain these technologies, setting trade terms that placed the elemental factions in debts impossible to repay.

"Retrievals are dangerous and never successful. We should not poke at our enemy while still licking our wounds from their last attack," the same elder says. "The elementals serving in the Upper were not forced. They all chose to go—"

"Under false pretenses. They volunteered, hoping to provide their families and our faction with tech and goods the Upper would only trade for servitude," Zimara says. "There was no true choice. And in the end, we sold our people for shiny machines and pretty fabrics."

Long before I was old enough to truly understand what was going on, the Upper began requiring periods of servitude to pay for the things we still needed from them. Now, I watch as the faction heads banter back and forth over the retrieval. They argue just as fervently as my own faction does on the matter.

Another elder speaks to support Zimara. "The Upper relinquished their right to those serving when they broke our agreement. All contracts were void when they cut off communication. Who knows what they could be doing? We cannot leave our people undefended in the hands of our enemies." The old woman's fingertips glow green as her voice raises. Thin vines snake up her arm, rising with her temper.

Regional agreements with the Upper started off amicably. All contracts held that once the length of service was up, the elementals would be free to return to their homes. Communication was open, and serving elementals could talk to their families via comm units.

But as the Upper gained more power, the prices of their technology grew steeper. The factions traded themselves into severe debt as the Upper raised its demands and lessened its output.

One by one, the factions grew enraged, refusing to trade any more servitude for goods, then refusing to trade at all. When the Upper cut off communication between serving elementals and their families, the factions took a stand, destroying the tech that had enslaved them.

The first elder argues with the old woman. "These elementals serve alongside those of the Terra Clan's Gold Faction, who still maintain an alliance with the Upper. Look at how they prosper, shielded from this damned war, while our faction dies beneath it." This sends the room into an uproar.

There are many hard feelings on the Gold Faction's decision to ally with the Upper. Each faction took its own time in the uprising, all entering separately. But the Golds did not join at all. Instead, they turned against the members of their own clan and region, debilitating the other factions by no longer trading their mined goods with us.

War did not start until we tried to reclaim the serving elementals. The remaining factions joined to infiltrate Central City. Though we failed to recover our lost elementals, the mission ended in the assassination of Prime Policymaker Nero. This was the initial act of war that has kept us locked in battle since.

The faction heads all begin to speak—profanities and logical arguments alike. The clamor turns into nonsensical rumbling of chaos until Corinth lifts a chunk of rock from the stone floor and slams it down, silencing the room and leaving a shallow crater in its wake. I survey the meeting room floor, noticing several crater-sized patches scattered about, and imagine this is a tactic she employs often.

"The Gold Faction plays a dangerous game," Corinth says. "They debilitated their own brothers and sisters through their refusal to trade while ameliorating our enemy. They will soon see they are nothing more than pawns quickly expending their usefulness." She looks around the room, pausing for any objections. "As for our faction, we will not entertain notions of surrendering to our enemy. Not when we have a genuine chance at success."

Mumbles float among those at the table, but none openly speak out against Corinth, so she continues.

"We have scouts watching the perimeter of Central City.

From our intel, we know the Lower elementals only serve inside the capital and usually only in the government buildings or lead policymakers' homes. We have not successfully infiltrated them, but our scouts assure us we are close."

An elder shakes her head. "It's too dangerous, we have already lost—"

Another elder cuts her off. "That's why we've asked them to come here," he says, gesturing to Kara and me. "Yes, it is dangerous. But with the help of the Smithers, we at least stand a chance."

"And what do you require from the Smithing Faction?" I say.

"Weapons. We will need blades made of magsidian. And reinforcements, should we fail and the Upper retaliates."

The old man lifts his chin, looking down at me as he makes his bold demands. I try not to gape at the absurdity of it. "The Smithing Faction cannot simply hand over magsidian weapons. They are dangerous and, in the wrong hands, could be catastrophic."

"So, the Smithing Faction cannot help us? They are unwilling to hold up their end of the agreement?" another elder says.

"The terms of the deal were not specified. I cannot promise something that is not solely mine to give. I can discuss these requests with my father and rally for support, but I cannot guarantee it."

"Oryn will not agree to anything until a union has taken place," another elder chimes in, and I know she is right. "When will you wed?"

My mouth runs dry, opening then closing at an answer I couldn't begin to give.

Kara's mother stands to speak up. "Cinis is here on a courting basis." Zimara looks at her daughter, but that does not stop the elders from bombarding her with questions and denunciations.

"So, she has not yet accepted?" They talk about us as if we're not standing right in front of them. They turn their focus on Kara, who shifts in place next to me. "And what are your intentions? How long do you aim to drag this out?"

She sputters to speak. "I-I—"

Her mother addresses the elders. "That is enough. We agreed to accept Cinis on a courting basis, and that is what we are doing. She will accept him when she is ready." But that does not end the discussion. The elders are unfazed by Zimara's show of authority. They press on with their queries.

"She still has not accepted succession. I am beginning to think we should appoint a new successor altogether," one elder says.

I take in a sharp breath. *Kara has not accepted her place as the faction's next lead?*

Zimara slams a hand on the table, and the ground tremors. "How dare you! Is that a threat?"

"No, simply an observation. Kara has neither accepted this union nor her role as our next lead. It seems that she wants neither. If that's the case, our faction is better off choosing a new successor who can form a union with the Smithers. At least then we can get on with it. Then, we might have a fighting chance in this war."

Kara shrinks beside me, and I want to tell her I understand. Although our reasons are different, I know what it means to look at people who are relying on you to lead and tell them you don't want it. To have the weight of their expectations in your hands and find you are unable to carry it.

Kara's grandmother stands. "Enough! There will be no talk of naming another successor. We agreed to give Kara time, and that's what we will do. Kara will announce her decision at the Autumn Equinox." She glares at each of the board members until they take their seats. She holds all the authority of a previous faction leader and no one dares to challenge her.

I glance over to Kara, who looks at me like I am a shackle and weighted ball—as she so often does. For the first time since my arrival, I understand why.

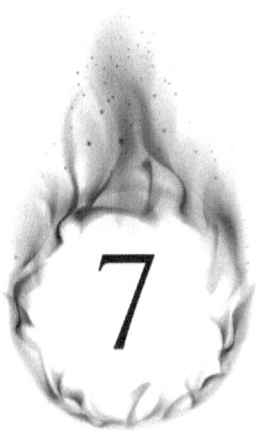

KARA

T HE AUTUMN EQUINOX.

The deadline burns into me like a slow-acting poison, counting down the days till my death. The time frame my grandmother has given me to announce my decision is only a short time away. This isn't time for me to decide. She's given me time to accept.

Rejecting my seat as the next faction lead and a union with Cinis is not an option. In the meeting of heads, the elders asked that we consider a new successor. The blow was both crippling and freeing. It's a stab to the heart, knowing generations of Nadir leaders could end with me. Knowing the bloodline which produced such brave and valiant leads could also produce such a cowardly and unsure one is the cruelest irony.

Although the elders may be harsh in their suggestions, they're not completely off-base. I know I'm unprepared to lead. And in this war, my mother could be called to Gaia at any time. It would be wrong to leave my faction with an inept lead for the sake of carrying on the Nadir line. My track record boasts no retrievals but dozens of deaths. My people don't deserve a leader who pales at the thought of taking another life. Who might hesitate when she should strike. Who would stand down in the face of an altercation because she is tired of fighting. A leader who could risk her entire faction because she is too crippled by regret and fear to be decisive.

I cannot continue the cycle of death and loss. The elders spoke truth: we've never executed a successful retrieval. In the years we've fought the Regional Battles, we've only known loss. Just this past battle, I led my own friend to her death. I cannot do this anymore. I can't see the point.

Caelum creeps into my thoughts, and I close my eyes, savoring his familiar smile and our family's emerald-green eyes. I cannot give up on him. Should I succeed in this, it may all be worth it. If we could bring him and the rest of our people home, I'd fight until my dying day. The weight of standing as faction lead would not be so unbearable if I was sure I could lead us to victory. To peace. If I could make us whole again.

And Cinis... My gut wrenches thinking of the way they

spoke about him and our union, as if he wasn't standing right in front of them. But while I wanted to hide under a rock, he did not waver. I suppose that's where his background as the son of a faction lead shows. We're used to such altercations with the head elders, but that doesn't make it any less mortifying.

I press a palm to my forehead. How could I have put him in such a position? My skin prickles with worry about what he must think of me now. Not having accepted my mother's succession isn't something I wanted to share with him. Not yet. He must look at me as weak. He may realize this is all a waste of time and go back to his own faction. It's alarming how much the prospect frightens me.

Since Cinis's arrival, I have treaded lightly, but my thoughts of him have only grown keener. Envy, gratitude, and admiration all battle to grip me, tinted with the hint of another emotion I haven't explored. He has a way with my people that makes him seem like a long-lost puzzle piece. Cinis seems to elicit joy and laughter wherever he goes and offers his smile generously, without expectation or artifice. He's become a sounding board for the pyros in my faction and a confidant and mentor to many of our warriors.

As badly as I'd like to give in to the allure of his warmth, I cannot face the judgment that will certainly come now that he knows I haven't accepted succession. Cinis has neither broached the subject nor sought my company since the meeting. This only confirms my fears. He knows that his potential bride is weak and her faction is unstable.

All I want is to talk to Caelum. To recapture a glimmer of what life was only a few years ago. Before I was called to battle. Before I was named successor. When we would sneak out to the greenery and make spirits from kelp fruit. Through my poison study—and Caelum's instruction—I practiced fermenting and spirit making. He, Rae, and I would sneak into the woods and get drunk off my latest batch of the awful-tasting liquid. We would talk and laugh together until the first rays of dawn.

After the meeting of heads, I went to Rae's house, hoping to get lost in the reassurance of my best friend. She wasn't there. That day, and every other day this week, Rae has been with Emrick. Warmth tickles my core, and I can't bite back the smile that lifts my cheeks at the image of them.

She told him about the baby, and they announced it to their families together. Emrick was ecstatic... Their families weren't so much. I understand, though. It's difficult to feel joy for a new life you know will be born into turmoil. With this war, there's so much uncertainty, so much danger, so much loss, and so much pain. But war or no, life goes on—it's funny that way.

I bide my time practicing with the orbises. They make me feel strong when I know I've acted weak. Today, I've left the blades behind. Wandering through the woodlands, I only want to get lost in my thoughts. I need to figure this out. I need to decide.

A tree burns at the edge of a nearby clearing, and I run to save it. Digging my hands into the dirt below, I command the soil to lift in a mighty wall that hovers over the sycamore. Pushing, I force it to coat the tree like a thick blanket, smothering the flames.

Cinis comes from the center of the clearing, where small fires blaze throughout. "I'm sorry. I didn't mean to—there's just no open space here. There are shrubs and things everywhere."

"It's okay. No harm done." When I pull back the blanket of dirt, allowing it to fall to the ground, we see this is not entirely true.

The trunk is severely charred, and my heart aches, for I know the tree feels pain. Placing my hand against the blackened bark, I allow my essence to flow into it, regenerating some of the burned pieces. This tree is old and wasn't able to move away from Cinis's flames like the others in the area. I look over to Cinis as he bites his lip, still consumed by fire, watching me regenerate the tree.

"The others moved. I didn't realize this one hadn't," he says.

"This one is old. The older they are, the slower they move—just like us. But she'll be fine." I pat the tree's trunk as she slowly lowers a branch to brush my cheek in gratitude. I move toward Cinis, and his fire recedes. "You guys don't have many trees near the Smithing Faction, do you?"

"No, just lots of sand. The terras there hate it. They scooped out their own small plot of land, and it's a constant struggle just to keep it thriving." He looks off into the distance, and I wonder if he's looking toward his home. "I never understood them until now."

"I can't imagine how different things must be for you here."

Cinis left everything familiar behind for this union. His pain tightens my chest, leaving an ache that compels me to reach out to him. I can't fathom the loneliness and desolation he must feel so far from home, in a faction so different from his. I want so badly to free him from his loneliness, to prove his choice to come here was not a mistake. I carefully graze my fingers along his warm arm, tracing the patterns decorating his skin before intertwining them into his. I grip his hand, linking him to me in a way I hope is grounding.

His gaze falls back on me, and his tight shoulders slacken. "How are you? You've been... *off* since the meeting."

I clench my jaw and look down. "About that. I'm so sorry for what happened there. I never wanted you to see us behave like that."

"Are you kidding me? You should try getting a bunch of elder pyros together to agree on something." He laughs, and the sound relaxes me.

"Still, it's not something I wanted you to see. I can only imagine what you think of me now—after hearing all of that."

"What I think?" His brows furrow, and the pitch of his voice raises with his question.

"You came here to form an alliance. To join with our faction's next leader. My family promised you that would be me, but... I'm not sure." I look down. I can't meet his eyes. Just saying these things to him exposes me in such a vulnerable way, but I owe him an explanation.

"I can't accept the lead when I'm not sure I can give my people better. I can't commit to running through the same cycles of battle, death, and loss. I can't lead more of my people to their demise while never returning any of those we've lost."

His mouth closes into a thin line as he nods. "That's why this retrieval is so important to you."

I sigh, resting my head in my hands. "If I can give my people this—a victory—that'd be something." It would be the slightest hope that this isn't all for naught. A hope to cling to, to see us through this war and into brighter days.

"My cousin still serves in Central City." I choke back a sob that threatens to shame me in front of the man whose kindness feels like something I don't deserve. "If I can bring him back, then my leadership would have done some good. Without that, what's the point?"

"I understand perfectly. We're not as different as you think."

I look up at him, but his eyes don't meet mine. I'm quiet, silently beseeching him to continue, needing to kindle the spark of hope that I am not alone in this struggle.

"I'm here now because I cannot accept the lead of my faction." He continues to look down. But the way his shoulders hunch makes him appear so exposed that I grip his hand a little tighter, just to remind him I'm here.

"My oldest brother was named successor soon after the Regional Battles began. I was so young back then, not even close to presenting at my true level. But because my siblings only presented as Level Twos, it was a safe assumption that I would as well. On my sixteenth birthday, I presented as an L3. Everything changed."

Cinis lowers himself to the grass, raking a fiery hand through his golden curls. I squint, amazed that the blond locks remain unaffected by the blaze. He looks in the distance to where I'm sure his true home lies.

"Our faction demanded the strongest lead. Because a Level Three presented in the Stallard bloodline, it didn't matter to many of them that my brother was already named successor. They called for me. And I couldn't do it."

I have never felt so connected to anyone as I do to Cinis in this moment. No one has ever understood the weight of a lead placed on shoulders that cannot bear it.

Finally, he looks up to meet my gaze, and a sad smile lifts the corners of his mouth. "You see, we're the same. I couldn't stay in my faction, because staying would only cause division when we need to stand united. So, I came here."

Sitting right next to me, he feels so far away, so lonely. He's been kind and patient with me, and I long to return the favor. I lift shy fingers up to his rich bronze skin, bringing them to the golden curls that blaze like a sunrise from his crown. I wrap my finger in one, wondering if it burns hot like the rest of him. He leans into my touch, and my loneliness retreats like a wave rolling out to sea.

His obsidian eyes sear into me as if they can see right through the haze clouding my mind. "Whatever you think came from the meeting of heads, I want you to know I'm happy I came here. And whether or not you accept the succession will not change that."

I bite my lip, losing myself in the sheer intensity of his gaze, feeling completely bared and stripped of all my guards. Slowly, he lifts a hand and rests the pad of his thumb on my bottom lip, gently pulling it from between my teeth. For a moment, I cannot breathe. The serenity I'd sought at the beginning of my walk unfurls in a warmth that touches every part of me.

The world stills as my heart slams against the inside of my chest. With his hot skin on mine, nothing else matters. Not the succession, not the engagement, the battle, my friends, or family—just this. Just here. Just now.

He brings his face closer to mine, and I do not pull away. I let him come so close that his breath tickles my skin, leaving a trail of chill bumps in its wake. His heat seeps into my bones and wraps around my core. As his lips brush against mine—soft and light as a summer breeze—I welcome the invasion, desperate for the moment of peace and security it brings.

"Yield!" A shout rings from the tree line, and I abruptly pull away from Cinis, breaking whatever spell my body and mind had been under.

"We really have to figure out this comm unit tech," Cinis mutters as he rises with me to see what news the messenger brings.

The young boy heaves, making his way to us, stopping just

short of reaching me, too breathless to deliver his report. I give him a moment to regain himself. He must have run all the way here. Anxiety prickles at my fingertips, as I know whatever message he brings is dire. When I can no longer wait for him to recover, I press him to continue.

"Well, what is it?"

Taking in one more deep breath, the boy speaks. "The heads—they're meeting." More heavy breaths. "The scouts have information. They found Caelum."

I stumble back, clutching to Cinis, who stands strong at my side. My heart thunders against my chest, drowning out the boy's breathy words.

I take off, not giving Cinis or the messenger a second glance. I need to reach the meeting hall and wish we had Cinis's glider.

He rushes behind me to ask, "Who is Caelum?"

I do not slow as I look over my shoulder to Cinis, who's racing behind me. "Caelum is my cousin. He is who I must retrieve."

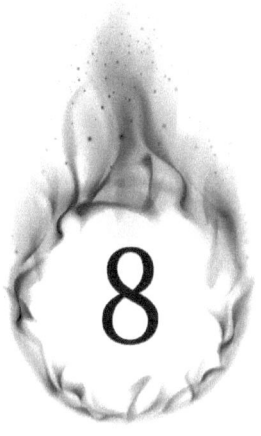

CINIS

I'M BARELY ABLE TO keep up as Kara races through the woodlands. She does not slow until we reach the meeting hall. The clamor of elders rings out through the open windows and door. We walk into a madhouse. Each head talking—screaming—over the other. Green vines snake across the table, and large rocks hang suspended in the air. All are fighting for the chance to be heard.

I hear Corinth's voice above the others. "We must act now." She slams a fist on the table. "Never have serving elementals left the walls of Central City."

Another head interrupts her. "That's exactly why we should

consider this. It could be a trap."

Yet another shouts over him. "We'll still be here thinking about this when our opportunity has passed. This is our best shot at rescuing the serving elementals and showing the Upper they're not to trifle with us."

The arguments do not stop. Words flow so quickly that I lose track of who is saying what, and what side each head is on.

Zimara stands to speak. "Caelum is in that group of traveling elementals. We cannot forsake him." The clamors of the room quiet as she continues. "We have failed so many of our brothers and sisters, unwittingly sending them to the Upper like lambs to a slaughter. We allowed them to serve in exchange for tech that quelled our greed. We failed them then; we cannot fail them now." No one argues.

She reviews the intelligence, which informs her that a small unit of Upper enforcers travels to the Outer.

"We must be swift in our attack. If we leave now, we can intercept them at the border."

I'm taken aback by the urgency. A retrieval alone is almost a suicide mission. Then again, one has never been attempted outside of Central City, where the walls are high and the enforcer presence is heavy.

"The report informs us there are approximately thirty-six enforcers traveling with a dozen captives. We'll take a small group of warriors so we can travel more quickly."

She is right. The larger the group, the slower the travel, and according to our intel, the enforcers have already left Central

City. The time it'll take to gather each elemental for this mission is precious. Time we cannot waste. The fewer going, the better.

"So, how many do you intend to bring on this mission?" they ask.

"Nineteen." She looks at me. "Twenty, should Cinis decide to join."

The table begins in uproar. "*Twenty?* We know they will have over thirty skilled soldiers. Do you wish to make this a suicide mission, Zimara?"

"We estimate only one Level Three travels among them. We'll have three in our group—four if Cinis joins. This will allow us to move more swiftly. And we hold the advantage of surprise. Once we free the serving elementals, that will add a dozen more to fight alongside us against the enforcers."

Her strategy is tactical and strong. The elders find little ground to argue it except for one.

"This will only work if Cinis joins," an old woman says. "Will you?"

I look to Kara, whose frenzied eyes stare up at me. I cannot let her down. This is my new home. These are my people. "I will."

Satisfied with my answer, the elders continue to challenge Zimara, like smiths hammering magsidian. They strike and strike until the plan is smooth and refined—flawless as a pyrasword. Kara looks up at me, her brows creasing. "You don't have to do this."

The gratitude in her words rings out above the false plea to reconsider. "I do. I stand with you—for better or for worse."

Her shoulders relax. Her gaze is soft and unassuming, and I know I will do anything to earn her trust.

Zimara's voice rises above the others as the meeting comes to an end. "It is settled. We leave now. We will gather the others and move out. We cannot allow the enforcers to make it to the Outer."

Kara stares at her mother, gaze as grave as the tomb. We all know what waits in the Outer. It's a prison region no one comes back from, and she is determined to save her people from that fate.

We leave the meeting hall quickly to gather the rest of the crew for this mission. Warriors, each one of them, are quick to comply. All are ready within a minute of being drafted.

At the edge of the faction, Zimara and Quarris unveil two old transporters. The rusty hunks of metal look like they've been raised from the dead. The two do not stifle their pride in telling us how they've restored the dilapidated tech. Despite their haggard appearance, they will give us the additional speed we need. It's the only way we could hope to intercept the enforcers in time. As my comrades squeeze into the two transporters, I invite Kara to ride with me on my glider.

"It'll sure beat packing yourself into one of those things," I say.

An elemental named Emrick nudges her shoulder. "Yeah, save a little more space for the rest of us."

She looks up at me, biting her lip, then releasing it. "All right."

She reaches out her hand so I can grab it and set her atop the glider behind me. The archaic transporters come to life, shaking and rattling. They're a far cry from the machines they once were, but they'll do for now.

We take off toward the Outer. I try to control my speed. The refurbished crafts cannot keep up. The journey to our destination feels like a race against time itself. I pray to Pyris that the transporters do not breakdown, which would end our mission before it begins.

Once we retrieve the serving elementals, they'll have to pack themselves into the already overstuffed transporters, at which point I know they will break down from the sheer weight, but the return home holds slightly more leniency than the journey there. Kara clutches to me as I speed ahead, scoping out the path, making sure we're not running into an ambush. I see we're clear and fall back to allow Zimara's pod to lead. When she slows to a stop, I know we're near our destination.

Quarris and the rest of our crew pour out the pods. They line up, standing in formation, awaiting Zimara's orders. Kara and I follow suit.

"Wait here," Zimara orders, moving several feet away from us to stand alone. "They're close. I'll scout them out." She fans her hands out at her sides, and the ground trembles. The soil slowly swallows her up, pulling her into it, covering her completely until nothing remains where she stood but disrupted dirt.

I look at Kara, urging her to explain what I just witnessed. To tell me where the plan is going now that our commander has disappeared.

"She travels through the ground." Kara looks fondly at the forest floor. "It's something she promises to teach me soon. She can travel the soil, connecting with the living things in it. She will do this until she finds where the enforcers are camped." I'm taken aback, amazed at the extent of her power. Although I grew up around some terras, none were Level Three.

We waste no time readying for battle. The crew sharpens their blades and camouflages their bodies to blend in with the landscape. The ground shakes again, and I watch as Zimara emerges from the land.

"They are near. Just as we were told, they travel in a group of thirty-six enforcers and twelve captives. They've stopped at the nearby lake to rest."

As we approach the Upper Region, its hallmark lakes and bodies of water have become more frequent. The enforcers will be a mix of air and water wielders, so it's no surprise they've stopped near their element to regenerate.

"The hydros hold too much power so near to the water. We must draw them from it." Zimara clears a patch of dirt and forces an imprint of the path we should take into it. "We'll follow just behind the tree line. They've shackled the captives, so we must be tactical in releasing them." She doles out tasks to each of us. We all play an intricate part in this rescue scheme.

"...and once the initial attack unfolds, Emrick can lead you three in releasing the captives." She points to a group of Level Two elementals, two terras and a pyro. "You must be swift. We cannot draw the hydros from their lake until the captives are free. Any delay in their liberation could cost us the mission."

After she's delegated all tasks, we move out. We creep through the trees, and I thank Pyris for our small, silent group. It's not long before we're looking over the lake. A short distance away sits our unsuspecting target.

9

KARA

WE TAKE UP OUR positions just behind the tree line. Mother slowly sinks into the ground. She will be the first to spring upon our prey, signaling the start of the ambush.

Cinis and I move to our stations. Our enemy dozes mere feet away. It's eerie to dangle death so closely over the unsuspecting targets. Our plan is to come in strong. Cinis and I, along with Tate, another L3 on this mission, will lead the ambush.

The soil in the middle of their camp rumbles, so subtle that our enemy doesn't detect it. Rather than the slow ascension she usually makes from the ground, my mother springs from the land like a summer weed, arms extended. From her fingertips, she throws thick vines to wrap around the necks of two Upper enforcers. Once we hear the snap of their bones, we make our move.

Tate and I spring from the trees, landing atop our unsuspecting victims. We take out another two enforcers before the rest of the camp wakes. As they charge from their pop-up tents, the rest of our comrades join in the fight. Elements fly on all sides as the battle ensues. I throw up thick walls of dirt to block my comrades from our enemy's attacks.

Hordes of ice daggers and swift winds assault the walls of my makeshift force field. An icicle ricochets off the side and impales my arm. I drop the barrier of dirt, clutching at my injury. Cinis wastes no time coming up from behind me, throwing a blaze of fire at our attackers. I tend to my wound while he and some of the terras go in on the enforcers directly ahead of us.

Blood pours from my arm, but I don't have time to summon the herbs that will help with clotting. I rip a patch of cloth from my shirt and wrap it over the puncture, hoping it'll buy me enough time to finish this battle before I'm forced to give it the attention it needs.

Once bandaged, I reenter the fight. Enforcers begin to overpower us. They still outnumber the meagre twenty warriors we came with. Emrick and the others have yet to free the serving elementals, who we're counting on to help us. A sharp wind knocks me over, pinning me to the ground. While there, I dig my hands into the soil, ripping it from beneath the air wielder that holds me. He slams into the ground and begins crawling toward me.

When I get up, he snatches my ankle and lays a fierce punch to my thigh. I double over but cannot afford to stay down long. I bring my elbow up to connect with his nose, and a faucet of blood pours from his nostrils.

"Help!" The scream comes from Emrick's direction. I leave the unconscious aero where he lies.

Racing to the others, I see they still have not freed the serving elementals. A massive wave emerges from the lake's center, and I know we have spent too much time near the hydros' element. Our plan was to move the fight away, draw them out. We can't do this until Emrick and his team free the captives. They have taken too much time. Now, we must fight the hydros on their turf.

I reach for my mother, who fights near me. Joining hands, we use our combined power to erect a massive barrier of soil to block the encroaching wave. The barrier will undoubtedly crumple upon impact, but it may buy us the time we need to free the captives. Only then will we stand a chance in this fight.

The wave crashes against our wall. Water flows on all sides, pouring over the top and sweeping us away. Cinis throws more fire at the hydros controlling the lake, holding them off while we regain ourselves.

I yell over to Emrick, "What's taking so long?"

"They're not cooperating!" he shouts back. I stare at him, unable to connect the words with logic. I don't understand how they could possibly be uncooperative in their own rescue mission.

Because we can't distance ourselves from the lake, we're forced to refocus our efforts on the hydros who control it. There's no escape now—we must push through and finish it here.

Enforcers surround Cinis, and I rush to his aid. He extends his arms, heaving in lungfuls of air. Reaching up, he seems to grip the sky. As he pulls down, a lightning bolt rips through the space between him and the surrounding enforcers.

I've never seen anyone wield lightning. He is magnificent, the electrifying intensity of his elemental device buzzing through the space. He surrounds himself in a ring of fire none of the enforcers can penetrate, recovering from the expenditure of his energy. They scramble. Meanwhile, Mother and I form a briar patch, manipulating the thorns of our tangled web to protrude thick and sharp.

Emrick is making progress releasing the captives. I let out a sigh; some of the pent-up apprehension coiling in my core finally releases. They'll come to our aid soon. We can win this.

A cluster of enforcers sees Emrick's efforts and charges toward him, throwing all their force into their elements. I reach for the orbises secured at my back, knowing now is the time to put them to use.

Mom extends her vines, plucking the horde of enforcers off one at a time before they can reach Emrick and his crew. She pulls them back and throws them into the briar patch. The thorned branches gobble up the elementals, snaking around and tangling them in the thicket.

Cinis blazes through another group, which means I am the only one standing between more charging enforcers and the captives Emrick struggles to free. I plant my feet beneath me, standing firm as I whip the orbises from my sides. I use the weapons to give my elemental abilities time to regenerate, pushing them forward with the vines that extend from my fingertips.

A hydro is the first to reach me. I bring my blade down, slicing through the arm he raises to strike me with. Before the blade can do any damage, the hydro liquifies his arm; the orbis flows through with no effect. A fist of water slams against my cheek, knocking me over. Another fist of water slams into my chin, then grabs hold of my throat, attempting to drown me where I stand.

I swing the orbis down, cutting through his torso, which he hasn't had time to turn liquid. The water falls from my neck, and I'm released, able to take in another breath. Three more hydros charge at me, and I lose no time pushing through the pile of enforcers. My orbises swing with as much force and vigor as an Upper machine. I'm relentless in my strikes. I do not care where my blows hit. I don't try to spare any of their lives, because I know their entire goal is to end mine.

As the bodies fall, I push through them, unable to focus on anything but the swing of my blades through the extension of my vines. When the last body drops, I fall with it, taking just a second to look around at the mess I've made. Sticky with fresh blood, I stumble over the bodies that lie in my wake.

Although we've eliminated so many, more enforcers over-take my crew. We had not anticipated having to wait this long for the aid of our captive brothers and sisters. I look for Emrick, needing to speed this process along.

"Get off me!" a captive yells, pushing Emrick away from the collar shackling his neck.

I rush to his aid. As I go closer, I recognize Caelum's emerald-green eyes. He has aged far beyond his actual years, his hair dull and the skin beneath his eyes sagging. His cheeks sink in to show cheekbones that were never prominent before.

"Caelum," I call to my cousin.

The closer I get, the more desperately he scrambles away. Caelum looks up at me, eyes wide and frightened, blood draining from his already pale face. His mouth hangs open in a scream that won't leave his throat. I freeze, remembering the blood that coats my body in a thick mess of crimson. I know what he sees.

He isn't staring at the little cousin who used to wreak havoc budding flowers in the winter when they should rest or pulling up roots to trip unsuspecting elders on their way to the meeting of heads. He sees a monster, as terrifying as any creature from the Outer, eager to snap up misbehaving elementals. The beast before him is far worse than any ghoul in the stories our parents cooked up to scare us into obedience in our youth.

"We're here to rescue you, but we need your help," I say.

"Who are you? Get away from me. Please, just let me go."

My stomach knots, twisting like I've just taken a punch to the gut. Air forces itself from my lungs as if it's been snatched away by an aero. I don't know what to say to the cousin who looks at me like a stranger.

"Caelum, it's me, Kara."

"I don't know you. Don't touch me. Please, let me go."

He couldn't have forgotten. Caelum's like a brother to me. He only left the faction a few years ago. Not enough time to forget me. My pulse races, and the lump in my throat expands as I heave in and out, becoming as frantic as Caelum himself.

"What happened to you? What'd they do?" I say.

Drawing closer, I look at the metal collar around his neck and lunge for it, intent on breaking any semblance of his servitude.

"Don't touch me!"

He fumbles and scrambles, desperate to evade my touch, but I pursue him still. I claw at the collar around his neck, needing to free him. Hoping that maybe if I remove the shackle that binds him, he'll somehow snap from the daze that has taken him from me.

Caelum claws at me like a wild animal, pushing from my reach. I grab for him as he stumbles back, but that only forces him to propel himself farther and faster until he falls into the briar patch my mother and I created.

"No!" I scream as Caelum impales himself on a massive thorn, the thicket branches snaking and whipping around to pull him deeper into their hold. I retract the briar with unnatural speed, willing my earnestness to turn back time. As if a quick retraction can change what has happened.

Caelum lies on the now bare ground, blood pouring from a dozen holes all over his body. I fall next to him, wrapping him up in my arms, begging him not to go.

"I'm so sorry. I'm so sorry." I say the words over and over, but Caelum does not respond. He does not look at me. And the way his emerald-green eyes glaze over, I know he will never look at anything again. I clutch his body close to mine as he bleeds out on the forest floor.

I look back to see the other captives frantically denying freedom, desperate to escape their liberators. They will not come to our aid. We are on our own, and as the enforcers overwhelm my crew, I know the battle is already lost.

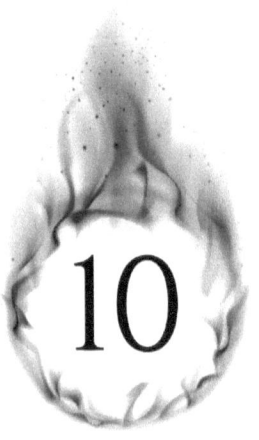

10

CINIS

F IVE AEROS SURROUND ME. They enclose me in a circle, stealing the oxygen that feeds my flames and gives breath to my lungs. I cringe as my chest tightens and spasms, fighting to take in air. I use my last reserves of energy to pull a lightning bolt from the sky, striking it to the ground beside me.

I miss my target, unable to fully control the elemental devise usually only wielded by Lightening Faction pyros. As the tide from the hydros' waves pool around our knees, the lightning seizes through the water and runs up the surrounding aeros. Their bodies shake and convulse as the raw electricity courses through them.

I scramble away, focusing on regenerating my energy. As I crouch down, I see Emrick and his crew fighting with the captives. I can't understand why they won't help us, but there is no time for thought now. Only action. We must get ourselves out. The extended time we spent near the lake, coupled with the captives' unwillingness to join our fight, has turned this battle into a bloodbath.

This is no retrieval. It is an execution.

A mask of water covers my face. I claw at it but cannot break free. I hear a loud crunch right before the mask drops. Behind me is the attacking hydro, a magsidian axe embedded in his forehead. Quarris runs to me. He reaches out his hand to grab my forearm. I grip him as he pulls me up from the ground. Bending, he pulls his weapon from the dead hydro's skull. I see it's the axe I gave him and have never been so grateful to have given a gift.

Tipping the bloodied axe to his forehead, he smiles. "The gift that keeps on giving."

A fresh spray of icicles hurls toward us. Quarris swings his axe, hitting off the first few before I throw up a wall of fire to block them. A scream pierces the air behind me as Quarris runs to charge at the attacking aeros.

"No! I'm so sorry!"

I turn to see Kara on the floor, clutching a dead captive. She's drawn the attention of more Upper enforcers.

"Retreat!" Zimara's order rings through the camp.

I enclose Kara and the dead man in a ring of fire. This only serves to deter the aeros for a moment. I push the fire out to expand the ring, forcing the aeros back. A lower-level hydro seeks to extinguish my flame. I heat the stream of water he wields until it is only steam that sprays across the aeros, burning them until they retreat.

I rush to Kara. "We have to go. Zimara called for retreat."

She only clutches the man tighter to her chest, mumbling, "I killed him."

The words jumble together. Her eyes look past me, her gaze unfocused, and she seems to have momentarily lost touch with reality. Our crew does their best to fight off the enforcers so we can make our retreat, but they still outnumber us.

"Kara, I need your help. We have to get out of here."

She grips the man. Tears cascade from her red eyes, leaving lines that streak down her blood and dirt-stained cheeks. I know if she doesn't help in our escape, we will bury more than the man she mourns now.

In my periphery, I catch Emrick suspended in the air, then slammed into a tree. I throw a ball of fire at his attacker, but I've lost too much essence wielding the lightning bolt. The aero covers my flame in a pocket of air before it reaches him, then extracts the oxygen so that the flame dies. He lifts Emrick up again, and Kara's head snaps toward them. Emrick kicks his feet, trying to evade the invisible rope coiling around his neck. His kicks slow as he loses the struggle. Kara's fingers ball into a tight fist that she raises in the air.

"No!" The high-pitched scream coming from her is unnatural as she slams her fist to the ground.

The world below opens, swallowing up the aero, along with the other hydros and air wielders surrounding him. Thick vines shoot out, reaching into the canyon to catch Emrick and some of our other comrades before they fall to the depths Kara has opened.

Collectively, we know this is our only opportunity for escape. Zimara pulls her vines up, carrying Emrick and two more terras, pushing them farther into the forest. Kara does not stop. As soon as her mother can clear our people from the area, she opens one crack in the ground after another, allowing it to swallow our enemies while Zimara catches any of our cohorts who tumble in behind them.

I draw on the last stretch of essence I have, to push rows of fire surrounding our adversaries so there is nowhere to run. As they work to climb out of the craters, I throw even more fire, hoping it'll delay their pursuit. Zimara wraps a vine around Kara's waist, pulling her out of the battle.

"We must go, now!" Zimara yanks the vines, dragging Kara into the forest as the rest of us retreat.

I stop running to scan the field, ensuring we leave no one behind. The man Kara held still lies among the flames. I can only guess it's Caelum. He meant a lot to her, and I know she will want to give him a proper burial.

I race to rescue the dead man from the blaze that threatens to singe his cold skin. Slinging the body over my shoulder, I push through the chaos and fire, retreating into the forest.

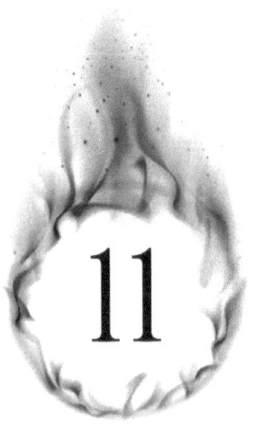

11

KARA

CAELUM IS DEAD.

My cousin's blood soaks through my clothes and stains every inch of my skin. It mixes with the blood of every other life I have taken today. It all remains a morbid reminder of the monster I am.

We run through the forest, racing away from the Upper enforcers, never slowing until we reach our transporters. Tate, my mother, and I pull what little essence we have left to form a temporary shelter. We erect walls of stone, camouflaging them with vines and shrubbery that will hide us should the Upper enforcers come in pursuit.

They won't. They've lost too many elementals and would still have to drag along the captives. But at this point, we can't afford to take any chances. I count my faction members as we take our rest. Thirteen. Only thirteen remain. This retrieval has cost us seven of our faction members. Seven warriors. I sink into a corner, burying my head in my knees.

Caelum is dead.

I killed him. Him and so many others. I lose track of the lives I've taken. They all blur together in a red haze. I'm repulsed by the monster I am, wishing even I could escape myself.

My mother sits beside me. She reaches a gentle hand to cup my head, holding it to her chest. She strokes the brown waves of my hair, shushing my sobs. I shouldn't be crying. It's shameful to make such a show of weakness in front of my fellow warriors, where it's my place to show strength, like my mother—like Cinis—unwavering in the face of death. But I am no leader, so I let the tears flow. I cannot hold them back anymore, and I no longer wish to try.

Mom hums a slow, gentle tune she hasn't sung to me since I was a little girl.

Mother, oh Gaia, send protection for me...
Ward off the evils of old...
Grant us a guardian, so we might be free...
Place us in their immortal hold...

The rhyme sings of the fabled guardians of our land, immortals gifted by the gods to protect us.

Her tune is so soft, as she hums against the crown of my

head, her chest vibrating with the song. Sobs crack open from my chest, filling the silence. So much has been destroyed. So much has been taken. My mother's fingers are steadfast in my hair. The hum of her shushes lull me until I'm out of tears to cry.

Once I've quieted, she starts to speak, though I wish she wouldn't. "This was not your fault. They changed him. Caelum was not himself. There was nothing you could do."

I let her talk, hoping that if I don't interrupt her—don't argue—it will be over soon. No words of comfort will change what happened—what I did. Instead of sitting here with us, Caelum lies on the forest floor, along with the seven other warriors who have fallen today. I'm sick, thinking of their bodies rotting atop the ground, exposed and unable to reunite with Gaia. I know we cannot go back to retrieve them. The stakes are too high. We barely escaped the first time and returning would risk even more lives.

I have failed. Failed my fallen cohorts, failed Caelum, just as I have failed so many others.

Cinis is the last to arrive at the shelter. Through my tear-blurred eyes, I can see he's carrying something slung across his shoulder. As he makes his way toward us, I realize he holds Caelum.

A fresh wave of tears falls down my cheeks as he moves closer. My mother and father rise to greet him. My dad holds out his hands, and Cinis gingerly places Caelum on his forearms. Dad holds him like a napping child, close to his chest. Caelum was his nephew. Cinis looks at me, his intense eyes searching my face. And when he opens his arms, I fall into them.

"Thank you." My chest feels as if it gapes open, emotion flooding in to take up the space. I do not have the words to express how grateful I am that he retrieved Caelum when I could not. And if I did, I'm sure I couldn't push them from my sob-choked throat.

During the retreat, my mother held me steadfast, dragging me from the battleground and flinging me into the forest. There was no time to go back for anyone. Not Caelum, not even our own comrades.

"I knew you would want to bury him," Cinis breathes into my hair, and another sob cracks through my chest. Raw emotion overwhelms me. There are no words for me to say, so I only hold him tighter.

Dad walks to the tree line near our shelter, and everyone falls behind him. Cinis does not let me go as we walk. He keeps his arm wrapped around me, as if he believes it is the only thing that will keep me upright. I hold on to him, because I might believe it, too.

While I walk to my dear cousin's burial site, grief and anger overtake me. Things were supposed to be so different. Today was supposed to be his homecoming, not his burial.

My father kneels to the ground, still holding Caelum. My mother crouches along with him, as do I, burying our hands in the ground. We search together for bilfium, each extracting our own from the ground, manipulating the leaves to grow long and wide. When we're satisfied, we lay them on the floor, and my father places Caelum atop. Mom and I take our time tucking the leaves around his now-cold body. When he's properly wrapped, we place our hands on the ground to open it up. When the soil splits for us, we part it just enough to fit him in.

Dad scoops Caelum in his arms one last time, laying him down in his final resting place. I say goodbye while we push the ground closed, sealing his body in.

"May Gaia return you to the land and breathe your life into all its greenery," my father whispers.

Mom and I rise as Dad stays kneeled on the floor. I turn away before he can stand. I don't dare to look upon his face—not now. Not after what I've done. It was my poor judgment that cost my cousin his life. I should have been calmer, more analytical. I should not have been so sporadic. I didn't properly assess the situation—and if I had, I would've known he was in danger.

I walk away from the shelter, waving Cinis off as he tries to follow. I need to be alone. I need to accept the consequences of my actions. Judgement calls like mine today make me unfit to lead.

My attempts to lead have only brought my people death and grief. Caelum would still be alive had he not crossed my path. I have failed him, Emi, and so many others. I will fail no more.

Caelum's death is my burden to bear, but the other seven elementals lost in this battle fall on my mother. She carries the weight in a way I never could. In a way, I fear I never will.

If there is any love in my heart for my people, I will renounce the call to lead and pass it to someone worthier.

I swear I will not damn my faction. I silently vow that before the Autumn Equinox, I will relinquish my claim to the seat and allow them to appoint the leader they deserve.

12

CINIS

IT DOESN'T TAKE US long to recuperate after Caelum's burial. The group is silent as they load themselves into the transports and prepare for the journey back to town. Kara lags behind, never saying a word. Her silence is so absolute that I fear I may never hear her voice again. When I help her onto the glider, she does not fight me. She does not fuss or insist she can do it herself. She concedes.

I'm no stranger to grief. I've lost count of the family members slain in the Regional Battles. I couldn't begin to guess how many friends have fallen in combat, never returning home. I don't internalize it, though. I release my pain through fire, through passion. When you hold everything in, it crushes you. I can see this in Kara as she crumbles under the weight of all that has happened.

Pain rips at my core, and my mind scrambles to find the words to comfort her. None come. I am helpless to save her from the invisible enemy waging war inside her mind. My touch will not bring her peace. There is nothing I can do to ease her pain. I can already feel her slipping away.

As she has so often done since I've arrived at the Healing Faction, Kara has secluded herself in the prison of her own thoughts, avoiding me like I am an open flame. As the faction grows nearer, panic clutches at my throat. When Kara steps down from this glider, I could lose her once again. She's only just begun to open up. I'm afraid to lose the progress we've made.

I wrap my hand around hers as it rests on my abdomen, praying it will somehow ground her to me, somehow keep her from running away. She tenses as we cross the entrance into the faction, their tribute to Gaia emerging as we move closer toward the town center. As the pods open to release our comrades, the townspeople rush to them—eyes wide and smiles broad—expecting victory. They silently count the elementals who emerge from the pods. Their smiles fade as the trickle of warriors slows, then stops at thirteen. Some look inside the transporters, hoping more await.

I'm not prepared for the horror that plays out on their faces when they see we have failed. I brace myself against the wails of family members of the warriors we lost. One woman frantically rushes through the crowd.

"*Robin.*" Her eyes are so wide they look manic, thick lines of tears streaking her cheeks. Her head jerks back and forth, searching the beaten and battered elementals. Zimara places a hand on her shoulder, not saying a word—only shaking her head. She catches the woman under her arms as she falls to the ground, crying the name of her dead love.

More sobs rip through the massive crowd, and their combined grief is overwhelming. Looking down to Kara, I know she cannot take it. I wrap my arm around her, shielding her from view of the approaching faction members. She does not push me away.

"Come on, let's get you home."

She shakes her head. "No, I'll stay."

We join Zimara and Quarris to hear the outrage of the faction heads.

"This proves we aren't equipped to win," an elder says.

"I told you to wait for aid. You do not listen, Zimara! Now, the blood of these warriors is on your hands," another shouts.

"We do not stand a chance against the Upper." Yet another voice is added to the mix.

Zimara stands before them, taking each blow as it comes to her. Accepting them as penance for the loss she has delivered her people. Although the accusations are not directed at Kara, I feel her crumble under each word.

I step forward. "You weren't there. You can't understand.

There's no way we could've prepared for what happened. The captives—they didn't... cooperate." I struggle to explain the bizarre scenario. "They didn't want our help. They didn't *know* us."

The elders take my words in as if I speak a foreign tongue, looking to each other for reassurance they aren't hearing things.

"What do you mean they wouldn't *cooperate*?" an elder says, as if the explanation could be any more plain.

"The captives fought us. They refused our aid and denied us theirs when we were counting on them to make our escape." For once, the heads are silent. No one has anything to say, because no one can wrap their mind around the absurdity of it. "I don't know what the Upper has done to the captives, but something isn't right."

The heads assess each other before countering me.

"We need the Smithing Faction's support now more than ever," a white-haired man croaks.

Kara's grandmother finally speaks. "Cinis, I implore you to return to your family and negotiate on our behalf."

My heart drops at the mention of returning home. Kara stiffens behind me.

"Our faction cannot take another loss. As their allies, we need their aid. Will you go speak for us?" It doesn't take a fool to anticipate the Upper will launch a retaliatory attack. The terra faction will fall without help.

"I will."

Kara shifts behind me. Corinth's shoulders relax as she lets out a sigh. I imagine she half expected me to refuse. She must not realize that I'm in too deep. "Excellent. You must leave at once. We have no time to waste. The Upper can retaliate at any moment, and we will not be ready."

"I will be there by sundown," I say and take my leave.

I say a quick goodbye to Kara and waste no time in readying my glider. There isn't anything I need to pack for the trip. I am going home. As my glider hums to life, my body buzzes with anticipation. It's only been a few weeks, but the ache for my home has never relented. I hop onto my transport and speed away, flying past the greenery until the vibrant rainbow of color turns to deep red.

I push my transport to speed over the familiar scarlet sands of my faction. The pull to my home is almost compulsive. By the time I reach my faction, I'm moving so quickly that the glider is almost unable to stop. I'm halted by two guards patrolling the border, but their eyes widen when they recognize me.

"Cinis, you're back," one says, his mouth hanging open.

"Yes, I need to speak with my father." They usher me in to the city that was once mine.

I head straight into town and do not stop until I reach my parents' house. I walk through the door, not bothering with formalities, knowing my father will be in his office. Opening the door, I see him sitting at his desk, and a deep relief washes over me at the familiar sight.

He jumps to his feet, fire igniting from his fingertips, preparing to attack. His eyes soften as they pass over me. The fire recedes, and his full beard lifts in a hardy smile.

"Cinis, what are you doing here?" He rounds the desk to meet me, pulling me into his embrace.

"I'm here on behalf of the Healing Faction. We are in need of aid."

His brows furrow, and a frown pulls down the edges of his beard. "And what aid do you request?"

I can tell by the inflection of his voice that he's surprised the Healing Faction is calling in favors so soon, but I press on.

"We need weapons and assistance." I take in a breath, shocked by my liberal use of the word *we*. Has it truly taken only a few weeks for me to lump myself in with the group? To adopt this new home?

My father scowls. "You ask no small thing of us, son."

I expected his apprehension but know I mustn't yield. I cannot let the terras down.

"We attempted a retrieval." My father's eyes widen while I explain how terribly wrong things went. "We anticipate retaliation from the Upper. In the faction's current state, the Healers cannot fend off an attack."

"Then Zimara should not have risked her faction in this way," my father bellows. Disapproval spikes his temper, illuminating the amber streaks of his irises.

"It was an opportunity to retrieve captives from her faction. Regardless of the risks, she could not allow the only opportunity to access captives outside Central City slip away."

"That is where you are wrong. You have much to learn of leadership, my son. You cannot risk the well-being of the many for the benefit of the few. A good leader *always* analyzes risk," he lectures.

"The risks were not apparent. There was no way for us to know the captives wouldn't help us escape. Regardless, what's done is done. We need weapons and warriors and are calling on the Smithing Faction for help."

Father's blazing eyes soften in the way they do before he has to deliver bad news. "And you expect me to provide this all before a union has taken place?" I knew this was coming. "Son, the last thing I want is for the terras to succumb to an Upper attack, but I cannot deplete our faction's resources and command our warriors to take up stations in a faction we have yet to hold stake in."

My mind races, trying to conjure up an argument that would persuade him otherwise. "A union will be made—"

"But when, Cinis? You have been there for weeks and have not sent word of the girl's acceptance."

"She has accepted," I say.

My hands fidget, and I clasp them together, afraid of giving myself away. I cannot tell him that Kara hasn't yet agreed. I must secure aid at any cost. "I was going to send word before the retrieval. We planned a union for the Autumn Equinox. We were to celebrate after the turning of the leaves."

I spin the lie faster than I can talk myself out of it. My heart aches at the intensity with which I long for the words to be true. When my parents presented this arrangement, I could have never imagined I'd come to wish for the union so wholly. "But we must delay. We must attend to the more pressing matters first. We cannot obsess over a union when the entire faction is in impending danger."

My father narrows his eyes, and I can tell that his lips press into a thin line by the furrow of his beard. His eyes are distant and considering. My heart slams against my chest, and I'm sure he sees right through my facade. His face softens a bit as he heaves a deep sigh.

"There is wisdom in this decision." A thick smile pulls across his face. "I am so pleased to hear she has accepted. Very well. I will prepare a band of warriors to station in the Healing Faction. They will be ready in a few days."

The coils of my body relax, relief flooding me. I could sing for joy if I didn't still have to figure out how to pull off this lie. The equinox is less than a week away. Kara will have decided by then. Should she refuse me, I stand to lose so much more than the girl I've come to care so deeply for. I stand to lose my faction's respect and my father's trust.

With a grand smile, Father slaps a heavy hand on my back. "As an early wedding gift, we will send you back with weapons, but I also require something from the Healers. A good faith gesture." He runs a hand down his thick beard. "We expect a shipment of medicines and boticin."

My jaw tightens. Boticin is a lethal poison. It is volatile and not easily handled. The terras guard it, rarely trading the capricious substance. They consider themselves responsible for the damage it could cause in the wrong hands, but I know my father will accept nothing less than what he's requested. I must relay the demand to the terras. This shouldn't be difficult, considering he is asking for so much less than he's providing.

My father and I negotiate the terms and which medicines I will request from the Healers, along with the boticin. Once we're agreed, he claps his hands together.

"Done. I will have the weapons you can carry secured to your transporter and prepare the rest to accompany our warriors in the coming days." He rubs his hands together like a child preparing to ravage a plate of ember cakes. "Now, we celebrate." His voice booms, laced with a proud joy I do not deserve. "We must tell your mother of the union at once."

His hand on my back guides me through the door. The rest of my family waits outside in the center room, no doubt tipped off about my impromptu visit. Father gives me a nudge as I halt in the doorway. Throwing his arms wide open, he bellows, "We have reason to celebrate. Cinis brings news of an impending union. The girl has accepted."

My family rushes me with their congratulations. Xanthe pulls me into a headlock, grinding his knuckles against my crown. Mother pushes him away, wrapping me in her arms. "My baby. My baby boy is getting married." She hugs me tighter.

Kenna chatters with Mom and Lana, already planning the ceremony's specifics. "We'll make an altar of fire glass so beautiful Pyris herself will be envious," my sister raves.

A pang of guilt twists my stomach at the false victory I'm allowing them to celebrate. I feel like a sham—the worst kind of traitor—lying to my family. But it is the only way to secure what the terras need to survive. I try to release myself from guilt, taking just the evening to bask in this fantasy.

Lycus makes his way over to me. "Congratulations, brother."

As he shakes my hand, he pulls me into an embrace, patting my back. I soak up his approval like I'm a starving man sitting before a feast. I know it is only because he believes I have solidified the union that will forever eliminate my threat to his lead, but I relish the connection all the same.

"Come, we must spread the good news to our people." My father's joy lightens his tone and causes his enormous frame to bounce up and down with his words. "Tonight, we celebrate."

The entire faction gathers in the town's center. They crowd around our tribute to Pyris, a tall glass depiction of the deity that shows her granting immortality to one of the pyro guardians. They offer me their congratulations and fill the air with an excited chatter of the solidified alliance. Father comes from the armory, silencing the crowd with a raised hand. He stops before the tribute to Pyris and bows, then rises and turns to me, holding out something covered by a thick pyrite sheet.

"The day you left for the Healing Faction, I had Thoron commission this sword." He lifts the sheet, and the collective gasps of the surrounding pyros pale in comparison to the thunder of elation blaring in my own head. He holds a pyrasword, newly forged and unblemished. I don't dare lift my hands to it until he gives an encouraging nod.

"These swords go to our faction's leaders." He addresses the crowd, "As my son joins the Healers, we become one."

My hands freeze. I cannot accept this. This is too great an honor, and it hinges on too great a deceit. He must misunderstand my hesitation, because his smile only broadens. "Go on, son, you've earned this. You have joined these two factions and will make a fierce leader."

I grasp the pyrasword as he thrusts it into my hands. A proud smile pushes the ends of his mustache to his earlobes. The feel of its magsidian hilt, curved to perfectly fit my grip, sends a thrill through my chest. I draw a flame from my shoulder, through the tip of the sword. It's not the same as when I'd handled my father and brother's pyraswords. This one is *mine*. Satisfied, my father brings his thick hands together.

"Praise Pyris!" he shouts, and the rest of the faction repeats it, starting the festivities.

I bring my ignited blade down to the pile of dry brush and timber surrounding the tribute. Lighting it ablaze, I am honored with initiating our offering to Pyris. Each member of my family follows, adding their own flames to the fire. The faction members follow them, all lending a spark to the massive fire dedicated to our deity.

We gather around to pay the goddess homage and offer her the fire from which all of us were born. It isn't until now that I realize how deep I've allowed this lie to bury me. I fear Pyris will pull lightning from the sky and strike me down for allowing tribute to be paid under false pretenses. But what's done is done. Whether or not Kara truly accepts me, I have at least secured the warriors and weapons her faction needs. No matter how short a time we'll have them.

The smell of roasted meat fills the air, and I salivate, practically able to taste the charred game. I've had very little meat since joining the Healers. The terras observe a predominately plant-based diet, and I hadn't realized how much I'd missed the dishes of my home faction, until the pits were lit.

As my fellow pyros dance and sing around the fire, I sit, watching the flames turn from yellow to blue to white at their hottest. I'm lost in my thoughts when a gentle hand rests on my shoulder. I don't have to look up to know it belongs to my mother. She takes a seat beside me, watching the flames dance.

"Your mind is heavy, my son. Unload your heart's burdens." She brushes the backs of her fingers along my temple and cheek, something she's done for as long as I can remember. It brings me comfort, and I allow myself to relax, just a bit. "Tell me about this girl of yours. Who is this young woman I will call daughter?"

I think of Kara and feel the furrow of my brow relax. "She is fierce."

My mother laughs. "If she wasn't, I would fear she could not handle you."

"She is strong—a Level Three. And selfless. She has such

a deep love for her faction. She carries the weight of all their burdens yet still thinks herself weak as she walks day to day with the bulk of it resting on her shoulders."

"And this humble girl, is she pretty?" My mother grins, twisting the curls atop my head.

"She is the most beautiful thing I've ever seen." The words escape my mouth before they register in my head. I break my gaze from the flames that roar before me, searching my mother's face. A wily grin pulls her lips so far back that I believe they will touch her ears.

"My baby boy, do you love this girl?"

And the answer is so truthful it feels like my soul speaks rather than my lips.

"Yes."

KARA

MERCIFUL GAIA, *I make this offering to you.*
I have spilled the blood of a fellow terra.
I have killed a child of vine and soil.
Benevolent Gaia, you are the mother of all land wielders.
I make this offering and beseech your mercy. I beg your forgiveness.

The ground shakes as a thick bilfium stalk bursts from the soil. Throwing all my essence into the offering, I will the trunk to grow thick and sturdy as I push it toward the heavens. The simple plant grows wider and taller than the colossal garganthian tree.

When it is stable and I'm satisfied with its height, vines spring from the ground. I draw fat, blooming roses from the creeping limbs, coloring them crimson for all the blood I have spilled upon my deity's blessed soil. I bud a flower for each life I've taken.

Crimson blooms sprout to cover every inch of the massive stalk, and I've lost track of the roses just as I've lost track of the lives. I give my best estimate, and the sight of so many pulls tears from my eyes.

I could say that war has made a murderer of me, but in truth, it may have simply exposed what I really am. Looking at the staggering offering, I pray Gaia will accept. But how could she? How can she look at all I have taken and not cast me away? Still, I command them to climb higher, so close to the heavens that Gaia might see.

I stand back, dwarfed by the obelisk of stalk and vine I have erected. I push the bilfium leaves to jut out and illuminate, though the sun still burns high in the sky. The glowing leaves against the full, budding roses make the tribute a spectacle to behold. I am unyielding in my drive to appease the goddess. Gaia can't ignore the offering, and I know she watches me. I only wish I knew whether she looks down with forgiveness or contempt.

I do not deserve her mercy. Gaia has blessed me with level and station, and I have made a mockery of her favor. I have squandered her gifts—gifts meant for a true leader—and dare to call on her for absolution. I cannot fathom why the nurturing and fruitful goddess would grant such abilities to a monster. Our element is the only one which births life; my goddess is the embodiment of fertility and vitality. How can a daughter of Gaia bring only death and destruction with gifts meant to spark life?

I am no daughter of Gaia. I do not deserve her mercy.

I leave the offering behind and walk back to town. Cinis has gone. He's returned to his faction to request aid, but doubt taunts me. I'm afraid he will beg them to call off the arrangement. He knows I am weak. He knows I cannot lead. He sees the foolish endeavor to unite with our faction for what it really is. I wouldn't be surprised if he doesn't return at all.

He's witnessed firsthand how pitifully I crumble under pressure. I have always been strong and confident in battle. It is the place where my cluttered mind silences and my sharp instincts and skill take over. Now, my sanctuary is where I failed in the only mission that truly mattered.

He knows I am the reason my cousin is dead. A true leader, Cinis brought our crew through the darkest of the battle and into safety. When the stakes were high and the odds against us, he did not panic. His decisions were not brash. Cinis is fit to lead the Healing Faction and deserves a like counterpart. If I had any honor, I would step down and allow a proper leader to take my place at his side.

As I enter town, it's impossible to ignore the buzz that seems to fill the space. Elementals clamor about, rushing to the town's entrance. I can only follow, pulled by the excitement and anticipation. When I've caught up to the crowd, their clamoring becomes more intelligible. People talk hurriedly, exchanging excited whispers that Cinis has returned. My heart leaps, and I hadn't realized how afraid I was of not seeing him again.

I push my way through the horde of people until I make it to the front. My parents and grandmother have already reached him. The back of his glider sags under the weight of two cargo bins hanging from each side.

When he looks up, his eyes fall on mine, and his mouth curves into a smile.

"The Smithing Faction has gifted us a small armory." He opens a cargo bin to pull out the finest sword I've ever seen. A flame extends from his hand and up the blade. I rush over to see the two bins loaded with more weapons of every sort.

"Even more will arrive in a few days with the warriors my faction sends to take up station here."

A breath explodes from my lungs as my entire body releases the tension I've held since his departure. My grandmother's hands clap together as my mom's chest seems to swell.

"How?" The breath of a whisper leaves my lips.

I am stunned that his faction would be so gracious in coming to our aid. Cinis only smiles and continues to tell us about the weapons and warriors set to arrive in a few days' time. I am more certain than ever he is the best thing to happen to this faction since the Regional Battles began. It's clear he will lead and allow our faction to flourish, as long as I'm not around to muddle his efforts.

"The Smithing Faction requires a minor trade in exchange for what they have provided." The elders straighten, apprehension throwing more wrinkles into their leathered faces.

Cinis continues, "They only require medicines."

I relax a bit at the simple request. Initially, the terms of this agreement included providing them with any medicines they may need.

"And boticin." Cinis lifts his chin, maintaining a firm expression as he reveals the second part of their requirements. The apprehension I originally felt returns, and I brace myself for the elders' arguments.

"It is too dangerous. Such a poison should not be taken lightly. There must be something else we can trade."

Cinis lifts a hand, already stepping into his leadership role. "The pyros' terms are fair. The Healing Faction stands to gain much in this exchange. My father will accept nothing less than the little he has requested. I recommend you accept his terms."

The elders counter, but Cinis is strong and unfaltering.

My mother steps forward. "We accept." She speaks for the others, and no one dares to argue.

"Excellent. We will make the exchange once the weaponry

and warriors arrive." After he's addressed the elders, Cinis closes the gap between us.

"How are you?" He lowers his head to meet my gaze. His voice is a soft caress against my skin.

"I'm fine." I wave him off, wishing he wouldn't fuss over me. "Thank you. I have no idea how you convinced your faction to allow us so many provisions, but I am grateful for whatever you did."

His gaze breaks from mine and falls to his feet as they shuffle in the dirt. He looks from the ground up to me once more. "It was nothing. There isn't anything I wouldn't do for you or this faction."

My gut twists. I'm touched by his devotion to a faction that is not his own. There's no way to tell how deep his commitment runs, or what he has risked on our behalf. It's a stark reminder that he represents everything right for this faction, while I have only caused hardship.

"I have to go," I say, before turning to walk away from the increasingly uncomfortable conversation. It becomes harder to face him the more I realize I must surrender my claim to lead.

He doesn't try to stop me.

I spend a considerable amount of time wandering through my faction. I walk the border of town until I find myself at the training arena where I practice my wielding, losing myself in the flow of dirt and vines. I release my essence into the soil below and allow the roots within to connect with me, so engrossed in my training that I lose track of time. Maybe I've been here for an hour. It could just as easily have been three or a lifetime.

Lightning streaks across the sky. A bolt shoots through a neighboring clearing. The sporadic flow can only originate from one thing—one person. Cinis.

I leave the arena behind to find him. I peek from behind the line of trees that encircle the open field. The toned muscles of his arms compress and release while he uses all his strength to pull something from the ground. Bringing my attention to his target, I finally make out what it is he's doing. Thick, red lava pools around his ankles as he works to open the ground beneath him, releasing the fiery sap.

I'm mesmerized by the sheer strength he exhibits in releasing the magma, in awe that he's able to do it alone. Though it is an elemental device shared between terras and pyros, just as ice is for hydros and aeros, magma wielding is typically a dual effort. Magma is too hot for most terras to wield alone and too deep in the ground for a pyro to access.

Cinis commands it as if he were born to. An illuminated lake of glowing lava forms around him, pulling past his ankles until he turns and finally sees me. I fight an urge to recoil behind the tree, realizing how silly it would look—especially since this isn't the first time. I emerge from behind it, my face heats, and I grimace, once again caught spying. His eyes soften, crinkling with his smile.

Shaking the still-dripping magma from his hands and feet,

he walks over to meet me. When he reaches me, he holds his hands out to grip mine. "Kara, I'm glad you're here."

"You're making quite a commotion. It's a wonder the whole faction isn't here."

Red tints his cheeks and he gives me a sheepish smile. "Yeah, my magma wielding is a little rusty."

"No, it's amazing."

"Thanks. My mother comes from the Fire Clan's Magma Faction." His hand drifts to the obsidian pendants hanging from his neck, and I understand his aptitude with the device. The faction sits on a massive volcano and is known for their products welded in raw lava.

"Well, I'm sure any of her faction members would be proud of the magnificent display you just provided." I gesture to the blackening rock forming atop the still-hot lava.

"Maybe you're right." He surveys his handiwork, lifting a branded bronze hand to grip the back of his neck. "But that's not why I did it." His gaze smolders into mine, and all thoughts escape me.

Cinis holds my hand tighter. He takes a step closer, bringing my palm to his lips, and this time, I let him. I do not command a thorn to puncture his flesh. I do not jerk away. I let his warm lips burn into my skin, and for the first time since Caelum's death, a spark jumps within me.

"My mother always taught me that the purest form of rebirth occurs after total and utter destruction." He moves his lips from my skin to look back at the cooled bed of lava.

"In drawing the magma from its resting place, it destroys the land and everything it touches."

I wince, thinking of the pain the soil felt in birthing the lake of magma, the scorching of the grass and greenery that lies beneath it. I pity their anguish. I mourn the loss.

Cinis continues, "But amid the death and destruction, new life will form. Once the lava has cooled, it will break down into the richest soil our world knows. That soil will give birth to stronger life, allowing more to flourish in its place than succumbed to its fire."

My heart breaks over the thought of atonement. I am pulled to the cooled magma. It sings to me like a siren, coaxing me to move forward. The desire for redemption compels me to reach my hand out and touch the still-hot soil.

The land buzzes beneath my palm, erupting with life. It is rich and pure and bursting with opportunity. Tears begin to well at the notion of absolution I do not deserve. I force my hand to pull away—to break from the hope of vindication for all the death and destruction I have caused.

Cinis kneels beside me. He brings a steady hand to my forehead, brushing away the waves that fall across my face. "This will not last forever. All destruction breeds new birth. All death makes way for new life."

I long to believe him. I'm desperate to escape my guilt and anguish, to believe there's hope for redemption and atonement. But I am not so naïve. Just as those who have died before and because of me, there are some things we just can't come back from.

I pull my gaze away from his, too ashamed to meet his eyes. He cups my chin, gently pulling it up. "Kara, you must release yourself from the judgment of your mind. I know it tortures you. The same guilt plagues me, but you are pure, and you are good."

I shake my head, as if the motion could expel the words from my brain. Tears blur my vision, and my chest feels as if it will cave in.

Cinis's hands fall on my shoulders. "You are strong and honorable, and you will lead this faction to better days."

"How can you say that? You've only seen me weak." I know he tells me lies. How could they be otherwise? He knows I haven't accepted the succession. I haven't been able to accept this union—to bind our factions in alliance. He saw me fail Caelum and so many others. He has never seen me strong.

I shake my head, trying to push the sweet lie away. His hand rests on my face, bringing it closer to his chest. In his arms, I feel safe. I feel comfort. Although it makes me look even weaker, I relinquish myself to the tears that spring from my eyes.

"I cannot lead this faction." The truth pours from my lips, and I cannot hold it back. "You will lead, not me."

"*We* will lead," he says, tilting my chin up once again. His eyes bear into mine, and I want to lose myself in them. "We can do this together. I will stand by your side through all things, Kara."

His confession comes out in a rush. "I'll admit, I was wary

of this agreement when it was first presented to me. Dreading it, even. But I never could've imagined how deeply I'd come to care for you and this faction. I see so much strength within you. It would be my deepest honor to serve as your partner for the rest of my days."

My breath hitches at this sweet admission. And for just a moment, I will myself to believe the lie. I forget myself in his pretty words and ignorant promises. He pulls me closer to him, running a warm hand through my hair, and I allow the sensation to overcome me.

"Kara, I'm in love with you." The words hang between us, heavy and absolute, like the obsidian pendants from his neck. He brings his hand to one of the black stones, lifting it above his head to rest in his palm. "I am yours. If only you will accept me."

The humility of his soft, onyx eyes—the vulnerability that plays out on his parted lips—is too much for me to bear.

Loving Cinis could be so easy. Believing his words could be as simple as wrapping myself in his fire and allowing it to keep me safe and warm for the rest of my days. I could let him paint a fantasy and run away with him in it.

I do not know if what I feel for the pyro is love. True, it is not all-encompassing. It does not overtake me like a wildfire or a mighty sandstorm. But it is something. It is a strong and steady pillar for me to lean against. In a life where the only all-consuming emotions I have ever felt have been grief and anger, I welcome the timid and unassuming flow of comfort and ease I find with the pyro.

As he places the obsidian in my palm, I close my fingers around it, bringing it to my heart. The action is instinctual, and I don't think about if I'm leading him on. I don't think about whether or not this is a promise I can keep. I simply allow the moment to sweep me away.

His hand cups the back of my neck, gently cradling my head. I lean into him, relinquishing all hesitation. As his lips find mine, I part them, breathing him in, tasting his fire. He is ablaze, and I have never been so eager to burn.

His scent is heady—smoky and laced with spice. It intoxicates me in ways an herb or drink never could. For the first time since Caelum's death, I feel no pain as Cinis's lips sear into my skin. Tears prickle across my eyelids at the raw emotion of it—the overwhelming sensation of release.

I push my lips back against his as his rough fingers dig into my hair. His mouth is urgent against mine, all-consuming in his hunger. In this moment, I need not repent for the sins I've committed. I have no burden to shoulder and no one to lead. There's only me and him.

He pulls me into him with each kiss—urgent and filled with need. Fire pours down my tongue and settles into my belly, and I only have to focus on the burn of it. No other qualms plague me. In this moment, I find peace.

I break from the kiss, practically gasping for air, pulling my bottom lip from his gentle bite.

I have gone too far.

Who knows the damage I've done? I know better than to abandon myself to him. As if my head was not plagued enough, my heart now holds its own set of burdens and anguish.

Cinis lifts the necklace from my palm to drape it over my neck, placing another kiss on my forehead. I want so badly to accept him. But I know it's not that simple. I would not only be accepting Cinis, but all that comes with him. The faction, the lead, the fate of every person in this town, all pressed into my shaky hands.

His destiny would be eternally tied to mine, and that is a misfortune I cannot place on him. I think of all the lives I've been forced to take over the period of this long war. I think of all the life that has been taken from me and know there can be no more.

It has never been more apparent to me than it is now that I must relinquish my claim to lead. I must leave Cinis and the faction behind.

14

CINIS

S HE IS MINE, AND I am hers.

I watch Kara wield from the magma soil for the better part of the afternoon. I marvel at the majestic flowers and shrubs she crafts from the rich turf. The ghost of her soft lips is pressed permanently onto mine. When the sun sets and there is no longer light for her to wield by, I walk her home.

I've never felt so weightless. I do not close my eyes under the moonlight. Sleep evades me. My mind cannot rest; I can only think of her. Her lips pressed beneath mine, the soft waves of her hair. The full embodiment of her element, she tastes like life itself. And she is to be mine.

I couldn't have imagined things going better. I've never wanted something so deeply as for her to accept me as her mate.

It astounds me how quickly things can change. Upon my arrival here, there was little I dreaded more than the thought of marrying a girl I'd never met. Finding myself stuck in a faction filled with elementals so different from my own. But I have grown to love the girl and the faction. I've found a peace here that only comes from the creation of something new. A peace I didn't realize I had been searching for until I found it—found her.

I don't bother retiring to my small room in Corinth's cottage. I spend the sleepless night looking up at the stars, thanking Pyris for her favor.

I think of the impending wedding ceremony, which will certainly be only a few weeks away. I can imagine my family transporting the massive altar of fire glass to the terras. The ceremony must be here. Fire and sand should not be all that surrounds Kara on the day of our union. She should be in her element. I can already see her, radiant among the bright green foliage. My mother will dress in the traditional onyx color of her home faction, along with my sister, and both will dance around the massive fire we will ignite as an offering to the deity that has blessed me so.

I clutch the obsidian around my neck as I gaze at the stars, relishing in the singularity of it. No longer two dangling pendants, one is with my match—my betrothed. And that is where it will stay for the rest of our days.

My mind wanders into the depths of night, racing until the first streaks of sunlight creep across the sky. As the sun rises, I let its rays sink into my skin, awakening the fire that lies beneath. I let it set my skin ablaze, completely consumed by the flame.

I rise and jolt into a sprint, hyper-energized despite the lack of rest. The flames die as I run into town, heading straight for the meeting hall. I'd agreed to join them this morning to hash out the specifics of our trade and couldn't be more eager to discuss. The news of Kara's acceptance burns at the forefront of my lips, but I keep them sealed. Autumn Equinox is only two days away, and she deserves to deliver the good news to her people after the turning of the leaves.

"Gaia has entrusted us to be the stewards of these botanicals. How irresponsible—"

"Gaia has not sent us warriors or weaponry. Gaia does not come to our aid—"

"*Blaspheme!*"

I've walked into an argument, which is all too common for this group. The way they banter back and forth is more akin to a pyro's volatile nature than a terra's. I clear my throat, stepping into the hall. The arguments cease as the elders turn their focus on me.

"Cinis, thank you for joining us." An elder squints his narrow eyes behind thick bifocals. "We were just discussing the terms of our agreement."

"Which is just that. Our agreement," I remind him.

"Five thousand units of boticin is too much. The quantity is unsafe. Reckless. Creating so much only to sit and wait breeds opportunity for misuse."

My temper flares at the accusation my former faction would misuse the poisons. "Misused by whom? Because I can assure you the blades the Smithing Faction provides are no less lethal than your poisons, and the warriors even more so."

"It is not the pyros I am most concerned about," he continues. "There is a reason we do not create our medicines and poisons in large quantities. Should the Upper overtake the Smithers, it would leave us exposed and vulnerable. They could take and manipulate the medicines and poisons we've created."

The man is right. The Upper has taken the Lower's creations before. One of Prime Policymaker Nero's first significant advances was in medicine. Somehow, the Upper replicated medicines that had, until then, been the sole creation of terras. This began the far and devastating fall of the Lower's trade structure.

We don't know what technology or knowledge allowed the Upper to extract and manipulate the poisonous and medicinal properties of the herbs and plants, but once they wielded that power, it was one less thing they needed to trade for. Followed by food, then metal, and weaponry. Their technological advancements boomed until we in the Lower became obsolete and desperate. Giving the Upper access to so much of the poison they have yet to replicate is foolhardy and reckless.

"There must be a compromise. The Smithers will not accept less than what they've bargained for unless you will decline some of the aid they so graciously supply."

The elders shrink back as if I've struck them. We all know they need every bit of aid my father sends, and after we've overcome so much to see this exchange through, I cannot allow our resolve to waver so close to the end.

I try a compromise. "What is the standard amount of boticin that is safe to produce and store?"

The gray-haired man rubs his chin. His eyes drift to the side, searching for the correct answer. "We do not need to manufacture and store large amounts of boticin. The Healers of our faction can fashion it on demand. But I believe a safe amount to store would be five hundred units."

I ponder this, pushing myself to form a resolution. Now that Kara has accepted me, these will one day be my people to lead. These decisions will be hers and mine to make, and we will bear the consequences, too. The thought is anxiety-inducing—being responsible for the lives of so many. I am hopeful that war will not claim Zimara and that she will lead late into her life. In times of peace, Kara and I could have expected to learn and study under her well into our middle age, but war has changed the norm.

"If you believe five hundred units is the most that can be safely stored, then five hundred units is what the Smithing Faction shall receive," I say as the man's thick eyebrows shoot toward his hairline. "The Smithers are only a day's travel away.

We will credit them for five thousand units to be delivered, five hundred units at a time. We will make ten installments of our payment until our debt is eliminated, adding an additional installment of five hundred units for a good faith measure and to show our appreciation for their patience and cooperation."

The old man goes to protest, but I cut him off, raising a fiery palm to the air. "Those are the terms." And as quickly as his mouth opened, it shuts.

Kara's grandmother speaks. "The Healing Faction agrees. All units of trade will be prepared and ready in two days' time, for the equinox."

15

KARA

ONLY ONE DAY UNTIL the Autumn Equinox.

I spent yesterday avoiding Cinis. I can't bear to look on his face now that I've made my decision. I know if I see him, even once more, I will lose my resolve. How easy would it be to forget myself in the warmth of his fire? To fall into his arms and let him tell me things will be all right? Even when I know it's a lie. Things will never be all right—not until I'm far from this place.

The town is abuzz preparing for tomorrow's celebration. Each year, we bring in the Autumn Equinox with the tra- ditional turning of leaves. Terra factions all over the Lower

Region spread to the forests and woodlands surrounding our towns, turning the leaves of shrubs, bushes, and trees, allowing the greenery to prepare for its great winter rest.

I'm saddened by the thought of missing it this year and comfort myself by promising to seek out the greenery too far from any faction's reach, taking it upon myself to turn it.

I remember, as a young girl, my mother leading me into the forest as I sat on my father's strong shoulders. She'd shown me how to coax the land to rest, my father lifting me high above his head to reach the branches. I'd watch the leaves change colors as if I'd stroked them with a paintbrush.

Most terras prefer the spring equinox. Where we coax buds to bloom and bring the life back to everything that surrounds them, but I've learned to appreciate the rest. I've come to know the importance of allowing things to die, just a little.

While I should busy myself gathering supplies for the equinox, I instead prepare for my escape. I say a secret goodbye at every turn. No matter where I go in this small faction, there is a memory rooted to all that I touch. My belly sinks at the thought of all I leave behind, but my resolve strengthens as I realize all I could destroy if I stay.

I know that once I leave, my faction will name one of the other L3s successor. A likely favorite will be Calise. Although she's a bit older, she is wiser and more stable. She will make a more suitable match for Cinis.

My heart rips itself apart, thinking of someone else standing next to him in a wedding ceremony. Staying here—with him—would be so easy. Loving him would be so easy. But it wouldn't be fair. Not to my faction and certainly not to him. He shouldn't be tied to someone he's constantly having to save—forced to make the right decision for both of us because I'm too anxious to make the call.

I grip the copper bracelet hanging on my wrist, the one Rae gave me for my sixteenth birthday when I presented as an L3. I know I cannot leave the faction without at least telling her goodbye.

I make my way to her home. When I reach the door, I hear Emrick's rolling laughter behind it. Warmth unfurls through my chest, and a smile tugs at the corners of my mouth. I'm so happy for my best friend. So happy she's found love and joy amid all the death and sorrow.

There's a danger in happiness during times of war. The danger of loving something so deeply that it will destroy you if it's taken away. That's why I couldn't let harm come to Emrick during the retrieval. I'd let my cousin and so many other comrades die in the heat of battle. But when Emrick stared into the face of death, I sprang into action. I don't know why my body and mind chose to react then—why I couldn't keep a clear head when Caelum's life hung in the balance. But I'm at least grateful I could deliver my friend's beloved back to her.

I land three heavy knocks on Rae's door. It swings open and Emrick's full smile greets me. "Kara, come in. We were just talking about you."

Rae laughs as I cross the threshold. "I'm sure you can solve this disagreement." She crosses her arms to look up at Emrick. I plop down on a cushioned chair, as I've done a thousand times before.

"Well, what is it?" I humor her, grateful for the moment of normalcy. The lighthearted conversation gives my mind a second's peace. For now, I can pretend this won't be the last time I see my best friend.

"I know the child within me wields fire, but Emrick insists that he'll wield land."

"He? So, you've already decided it's a boy?"

"Yes," they say in unison. Rae laughs and continues. "It's definitely a boy."

"And how could you possibly know that?"

"Mother's intuition." She shrugs. "The same mother's intuition that tells me he will be a pyro." She sticks her tongue out at Emrick.

"Well, you can't argue with mother's intuition," I tease him as he pulls Rae into his arms, lifting her up to land a kiss on her brow.

"Whatever he is, he will be perfect," Emrick says between kisses.

I smile, looking away, doing my best to give them privacy. Tears sting my eyes at the mention of a child I will never meet. I'm struck by the thought that I won't be next to Rae when she delivers her son. But Emrick will be more than enough, standing in my place. As Healers, we're all well equipped to deliver babies, and he will be all she needs.

As Rae and Emrick sway, tangled in each other's arms, I laugh at their love-struck gaze. I know it's time for me to take my leave.

When I stand, Rae breaks away from Emrick, catching my hand. "You're leaving?"

The question knocks the breath from my lungs. She says it as if she *knows*, but that is impossible.

"Yeah. I just came by to check in. I still have some prep to do before tomorrow's celebration."

She looks down, still holding my hand, then back up at me. "Okay, but we'll still bring in the equinox together, right?"

Each year, Rae accompanies me as we go through the forest. Because she is not a terra, she can't take part in the turning ceremony, but that's never kept her from tagging along.

"Oh, I... I thought you'd be going with Emrick this year."

She turns and makes a show of rolling her eyes. "Nope, I'm sticking with my Level Three for this one." She links her arm with mine and sends a teasing smile over her shoulder to Emrick.

I turn to look at her one last time.

"It's a date," I lie, pulling her into my arms, hugging her so tightly I might still be able to feel this embrace long after I'm gone.

When we pull away, she looks at me, raising a brow. "I'll see you tomorrow."

The statement sounds like a question. I only nod, because

I can't force another lie past my lips, then turn to leave her cottage.

The day goes by too quickly as I scramble to gather all my supplies. It's a welcome distraction to keep my mind from settling on what I plan to do.

I'll escape in the dead of night while all the other elementals rest in anticipation of the equinox. I've already scouted a route that will take me out of the faction. I know I can slip away without anyone noticing. If I stick to the woodland's outskirts, I can get far enough, fast enough, to outrun anyone who would come looking for me.

I give my mother and father a kiss goodnight before retiring to my room. They can't know I've kissed them for the last time. I close the door before the tears spill, giving me away. I mourn the loss of my faction and family before I'm even gone and try to find resolve in the nobility of sacrificing all that I love for the greater good.

Before lying down in my bed, I check beneath it for the bag of supplies I've procured throughout the day. There isn't much I'll need before reaching my destination. My land wielding is strong enough to sustain me. I can produce all the food I'll need, and albeit minimal, I can produce shelter as well.

I plan to run as far west as my feet can take me, disappearing in a far-off terra faction. I'll go far enough away that no one will recognize my face—so far that Corinth and Zimara won't be household names. I want to be somewhere secluded—far enough from town to be unbothered but close enough to trade for necessities.

I welcome the loneliness, the isolation it promises. I accept it as my penance for abandoning all that I love.

Lying down in bed, I wait to pass the next few hours before deserting my faction. I clutch the obsidian pendant hanging around my neck. It bears a disproportionate weight down on my chest. A better woman would leave it for Cinis so he might find closure, confident I will never return. Leave it so that he might gift it to a worthier partner, the woman he will inevitably make his wife.

But I am not a better woman. And I will not relinquish the pendant. I'm about to leave so much behind that I can't bear not having at least one thing of his to keep. To hold dear to me always.

So, I lie there, clutching the stone above my heart, until it is time for me to run.

CINIS

I T'S THE DEAD OF night, and the Autumn Equinox is upon us. There are only a few hours until dawn, and I know my father's warriors have already begun their journey to us. The lie's crushing weight has lifted from my chest. Kara has accepted me, and I can meet my people with good news rather than dishonor.

They travel as a large group and will not reach us until well past midday. My body buzzes with anticipation of what the day promises to bring.

A shattering *boom* jolts me from my thoughts and out of bed. I race to the door, only to fall again, knocked down by a blast of arctic wind that shatters the cottage's windows. Corinth rushes from her room, but when she reaches me, I've already donned the sheath that holds my pyrasword.

She's a step behind me when I pull the door open, and my body stiffens. I feel the blood freeze in my veins as I take in the scene before me.

Water pools around our ankles, rushing into Corinth's home. I look out to see a mass of Upper soldiers attacking houses on every side of us and realize all my planning and preparation was for naught. This is their retaliation. We are under attack.

The weeks I'd hoped we'd have to strengthen and prepare will not come. They attack us here, now. Never in my wildest dreams could I have imagined they would counter so brutally. They did not send a small crew of elementals to challenge us outside the faction. They did not wait for our warriors to venture into battle. The Upper sent an entire brigade to decimate a civilian town while the rest of the world sleeps.

I don't have to run far from Corinth's doorstep to meet an enemy's element. A rope of water wraps around my waist. Flames already engulf my hand by the time I reach up to grab my pyrasword. As I pull it from the sheath, my flame licks up the blade, so hot it burns blue.

I grip the hilt with both hands, bringing the sword down in a swift thrust, slicing through the hydro standing before me. The intense heat of my blade cauterizes the man's wounds as it cuts. There is no spray of blood, only the sloshing sound of his neck and shoulder sliding from his lower body.

Dozens of Upper soldiers pour into the town's center. They don't discriminate in their victims, fighting Level Ones and Twos, young and old. The town is a madhouse of frantic and wayward elements thrown about in no organized fashion. This makes it easy for Upper soldiers to overpower the unsuspecting healer elementals.

I can't focus my mind through the burning questions that swarm me. Though we've fought the Regional Battles for years, neither side has ever crossed *this* line. Neither has committed an act so egregious as to attack a civilian town. We couldn't have anticipated this. Our lack of preparedness is clear and costing us dearly.

Wall after wall of water slams into me, extinguishing the flames I've drawn from my hands to cover the sword. I push heat through my body, drying myself, turning the dampness into steam. I generate one large fireball after another, hurling them at my enemy, showing no mercy to the elementals who stand before me. I throw so much power into the fireballs they burn white, incinerating each target upon contact.

My rage compounds as I think of all this battle will cost. All that I've risked getting to this point. As the Uppers further their attacks, it becomes clearer that it was all for nothing. The weapons, the soldiers, the alliance... Kara.

My first impulse is to find her. To make sure she is all right and protect her in any way I can. I would lay down my life without hesitation if it meant sparing hers. But Kara doesn't need my protection. She is strong. She is powerful. And she can hold her own. I know my place is here, guarding the group of L1 wielders not trained in combat. Trying to save the children and elderly who can't defend themselves against skilled Upper soldiers.

I crowd them together. "Find Corinth. We must get you out of here."

The unrelenting brigade is quickly gaining ground. Although the faction of land and fire wielders far outnumbers them, it doesn't matter. Just a handful of trained soldiers will overtake us with sickening ease.

I hear Emrick's voice boom through the space. He shouts orders to elementals I recognize as Healer warriors. He wields his own element against the brigade, but this is different from any battle he's led before.

Combat does not consume us. We do not fight to gain ground. We are fighting to protect the innocent noncombatants who scurry from our attackers. Rather than giving their hearts to the battle, these warriors' skills are dulled by the raw desperation to protect the ones they hold dear. The effort to defend our faction is futile. We must move on to saving as many as we can.

A massive obelisk of dirt and rock stretches high into the sky. It looms far above the roof and treetops, and I know it must be Corinth. I point to the towering structure, knowing it will break apart to attack its enemy at any moment.

"There," I say, directing the group of L1s. "Go there. You'll find Corinth. Tell her she must gather as many elementals as she can and take you out of the city."

Their weary eyes lock with mine. They know how daunting it will be to cross the town through such an uproar. But I can't accompany them. I must stave off the Upper soldiers so they might stand a chance at escape.

Losing Corinth will wound us deeply. There are so few Level Threes in the faction that losing one so strong will cripple our defense. But we only need to guard the faction long enough for the others to get away. We only need our warriors to hold their soldiers off until we can get them out.

The group moves toward Corinth's location. Older elementals lead, covering and protecting the children. One lingers. A young, red-headed pyro. The boy hasn't even hit puberty, but his fists ball in small flames.

"Paeta, go with them, now."

"No, I'm going to fight." The boy has heart. It's not only fire that engulfs his hands. The boy has a fire that burns deep within. Still, I can't let him stay.

"Damn it, Paeta, I said to go now. That's an order."

He only balls his fist tighter and stands taller, puffing his chest as if to challenge me. I'm so moved by his bravery that I almost forgive his stubbornness.

Bending over, I rest a hand on his shoulder. "You must go with the others. You're probably the bravest and strongest fire wielder in that group. Corinth will need your help to protect them, and they'll need a strong pyro to stand guard. Can you do that for me?"

The boy stiffens, seemingly pleased to play protector. He lifts his head to nod as a block of ice encloses him. An air wielder throws more ice and begins closing me in as well. I push flames from my core, incinerating myself and melting the element. With a flash of heat, I melt the sheet covering Paeta and point to the fleeing group.

"Go, now!" I say, hurling a heat wave to the aeros surrounding us.

The wave knocks them to their backs, and Paeta scrambles away. More aeros flood into the area around me, throwing ice and daggers aimed at my vital organs. I push more flames to cover my body and sword in a white-hot blaze that melts any ice before it can even touch my skin.

I charge my enemy, slicing the fiery blade through throat and limb. My sword finds itself wedged in a man's hip, no doubt caught through bone. After a quick tug, I know it's lodged in there good. Wincing, I drop the pyrasword and man, leaving them both behind, knowing my hands will be of more use to me free. I silently swear to come back for the blade should I make it through the battle alive.

Hydros throw streams of water in an attempt to extinguish my flames, but they burn too hot. The water turns to steam that burns and coats the surrounding soldiers. I reach my free hand up to the sky and pull down a lightning bolt. I'm not precise with my aim, though the device is powerful enough to take out the surrounding soldiers in one strike. The earth quakes and the ground splits as I thrust the bolt of electricity through my opponents, not caring how much destruction I cause. I do not conserve my essence. I let it all flow out into the element I wield. I know I'll have no use for it much longer.

Upper soldiers grab and bind the people of this town by the handful. Our faction is lost.

A swirling turbine of dust and rocks wreaks havoc on a cluster of soldiers nearby. I look to see Kara is the center of that chaos. She calls out for me, and I rush to her, extinguishing my flames as I approach. My hands draw to her like metal to magnetite. I scan her body, making sure she isn't injured, then pull her close. Immediate relief floods me, accompanied by another set of emotions I do not have the time to decipher.

"You're all right," I breathe into her hair.

She grips me tighter, and I want nothing more than for the world to fall away as I hold her in my arms.

"What's happening? Why are they here?" she pleads as if I have an answer.

"I don't know. All I know is that they're taking elementals, caging them, and loading them onto transporters." I surround us in a ring of fire that provides some protection from the ensuing elements, if only for a moment. Her hands hold steadfast to my waist, and I grip her even tighter to me. "We have to get the others out."

She tilts her head back, looking up at me to nod. Knowing just as well as I that the battle is lost.

"My grandmother," she says.

I nod, and we run as the ensuing hydros penetrate our protective shield of fire.

We race to the edge of the faction, where we find a massive garganthian tree manipulated to grow double its natural size. The branches of the tree swoop down, throwing Upper soldiers from their path. Thick roots shake the ground as they shoot up to slap down over the hydros who close in, and I know we've found Corinth. She uses all her power to stave them off but won't be able to hold her ground for much longer.

"Open the soil," I call to Kara, knowing just how to eliminate the threat. She doesn't hesitate in dropping to the ground, sinking her hands deep into the dirt. As the land parts, I can easily pull the molten lava bubbling from its core.

Magma flows from the cracks in the land to pool over Kara's hands. I wince at the pain she must feel against an element so harsh and not her own. She doesn't let on to her suffering; her hands remain still and steadfast beneath the flow. I push the magma across the way to splatter and cover the hydros and aeros in pursuit. Their elements cool the magma, turning it into rock that encases them.

Kara rushes toward her grandmother as Corinth calls out to her.

"Grandma, you have to get them out of here." Kara gestures to the large and growing group of elementals her grandmother has corralled.

"Yes. There are more waiting outside town. But we have

nowhere to go."

My soul swells in a small triumph that even more elementals will make it to safety. I do not hesitate. I know where she can lead them. "Take them to my faction. Pyro warriors travel here now. Meet them on the route, and have them escort you to the Smithing Faction."

This battle is done. We cannot use the Smithing warriors; we've lost too many of our own. Asking them to fight now that so many terras have been captured will only ensure their demise.

"They will take you in. Tell my father I've sent you, and give him this." My hands move to the pendant hanging from my neck. The joy of wearing it while my betrothed wore its match was short-lived but fulfilling. As much as it pains me to part with the stone, I know the message it sends to my mother and father will be clear.

Kara takes in a breath, then turns to me. "Cinis, you have to go. You can't stay here. There's no way for us to win this. Lead them back to your faction, and return home." Her words come out rushed and stammering.

The only thing that would plague me more than parting from the pendant is parting from her. I made a vow, a promise that I am hers and she is mine. I would never leave her side. I bring my hands to wrap around hers. "I'm staying right here."

She squeezes her eyes shut, flinching as if struck. She quickly recovers herself, then yells to her grandmother, "Go now!"

A hydro pierces the ground with jutting streams of scalding

water. Geysers shoot out one after another, surrounding us and hiding the water wielders who control them. I heat the streams until they turn to steam that reveals the hydros they shield.

Kara moves to focus her efforts on an ensuing aero and vanishes from sight. More hydros surround me, and I'm once again encased in flames. They are swift in their attack. Chains of water wrap around me. Liquid ropes squeeze my neck and force their way down my windpipe. I struggle for breath, heating the water as quickly as I can, choking on the steam that bubbles from my throat.

Just as I've cleared one attack, blocks of ice slam into my head, knocking me from the ground. My vision spots in and out, and I can no longer see my opponents. Reaching a hand to the sky, I pull lightning from it, throwing it down to the aero I know is near.

As my vision comes back into focus, I reach for another bolt, but the burst of elemental power I have allowed to escape me is too great. I'm growing weary and weak. My lightning stalls before it strikes, and the hydros waste no time slapping my face with water that wraps around to suffocate me faster than I can evaporate it.

As my hand lifts once more to pull lightning from the air, the flame cools, and my arm slams back to the floor. Ice encases my fist and creeps up across my arm. It moves across my body, and I'm unable to melt it.

More aeros close in on me, burying me deep in their element.

Thick walls of ice cover every inch of my skin until I can't move. I push heat from my core, but rather than a roaring flame, all I can generate is the flicker of a spark that quickly dies.

An older aero moves to me, lifting his upper lip in a sneer. "You've been captured, pyro. Yield."

"Never."

The man looks back at his hovering lackeys with a sick grin that contorts his bloodied face. When he turns back to me, his foot lifts simultaneously. He brings it down to slam into my head, knocking me back.

The last thing I feel is the trickle of blood before everything fades to black.

Does Cinis survive the attack? Does Kara run? Who is the commander leading the enemy army, and how does his destiny intertwine with Cinis and Kara's?
Find out here:
http://bit.ly/OCABM

Thank you for reading, Of Chaos and Fire. I truly hope you enjoyed Cinis and Kara's story and would consider leaving a review so that you can help other readers find their story.

Want to connect? Visit me here:

https://bit.ly/MegLT

Acknowledgements

This book would not have been possible without the love and support of so many people. Thank you to my husband for always supporting my dreams, no matter how fanciful. Thank you to my mother for always encouraging me to reach for the stars. Thank you to my beta readers who painstakingly read through each unedited and incomplete version of this manuscript to help me create the final piece you have before you. Thank you to my editors, who are story, syntax, and proofreading geniuses. And thank *you*, for taking a chance on me and the work I've poured my heart into.

ABOUT THE AUTHOR

Meghan Rhine is a product of the generation who sent count-less letters to the Hogwarts Admissions Office, fell in love with sparkly vampires, jumped onto Dauntless trains, and volun-teered as tribute in the reaping. She now resides deep in the bayous of Louisiana, where she reigns as queen of the wild things (three adorable little wild things). There, with her hus-band and three sons, Meghan lives her life fueled by coffee and sarcastic humor, one day hoping to work for the secret part of the government in charge of alien interactions.

Visit her on the web, and get free books, first looks, giveaways, and more, by subscribing to her mailing list at
https://bit.ly/MegLT

www.ingramcontent.com/pod-product-compliance
Lightning Source LLC
Chambersburg PA
CBHW051947170626
46808CB00007B/2519